MERCER MAY
CRITTER KIDS® ADV

MW01121795

THE PRINCE
A GRAPHIC NOVEL ADVENTURE

School Specialty Publishing

Copyright © 2006 © 1995 Mercer Mayer Ltd.
Text for Page 32 © 2006 School Specialty Publishing.
Published by School Specialty Publishing, a member of the School Specialty Family.
A Big Tuna Trading Company, LLC/J. R. Sansevere Book

Critter Kids is a Registered Trademark of Mercer Mayer Ltd. All rights reserved.
Printed in the United States of America. All rights reserved. Except as permitted under the United States
Copyright Act, no part of this publication may be reproduced or distributed in any form or by any means,
or stored in a database retrieval system, without prior written permission from the publisher. Send all inquiries to:
School Specialty Publishing, 8720 Orion Place, Columbus OH 43240-2111

Written by Erica Farber/J. R. Sansevere
Special thanks to Paul Binski, Department of History of Art, University of Manchester, England

ISBN 0-7696-4767-7

1 2 3 4 5 6 7 8 9 10 PHX 11 10 09 08 07 06

The **MIDDLE AGES**, or the medieval period, took place between 400 and 1400 A.D. The word *medieval* comes from two Latin words, *medium* ("middle") and *aevum* ("age").

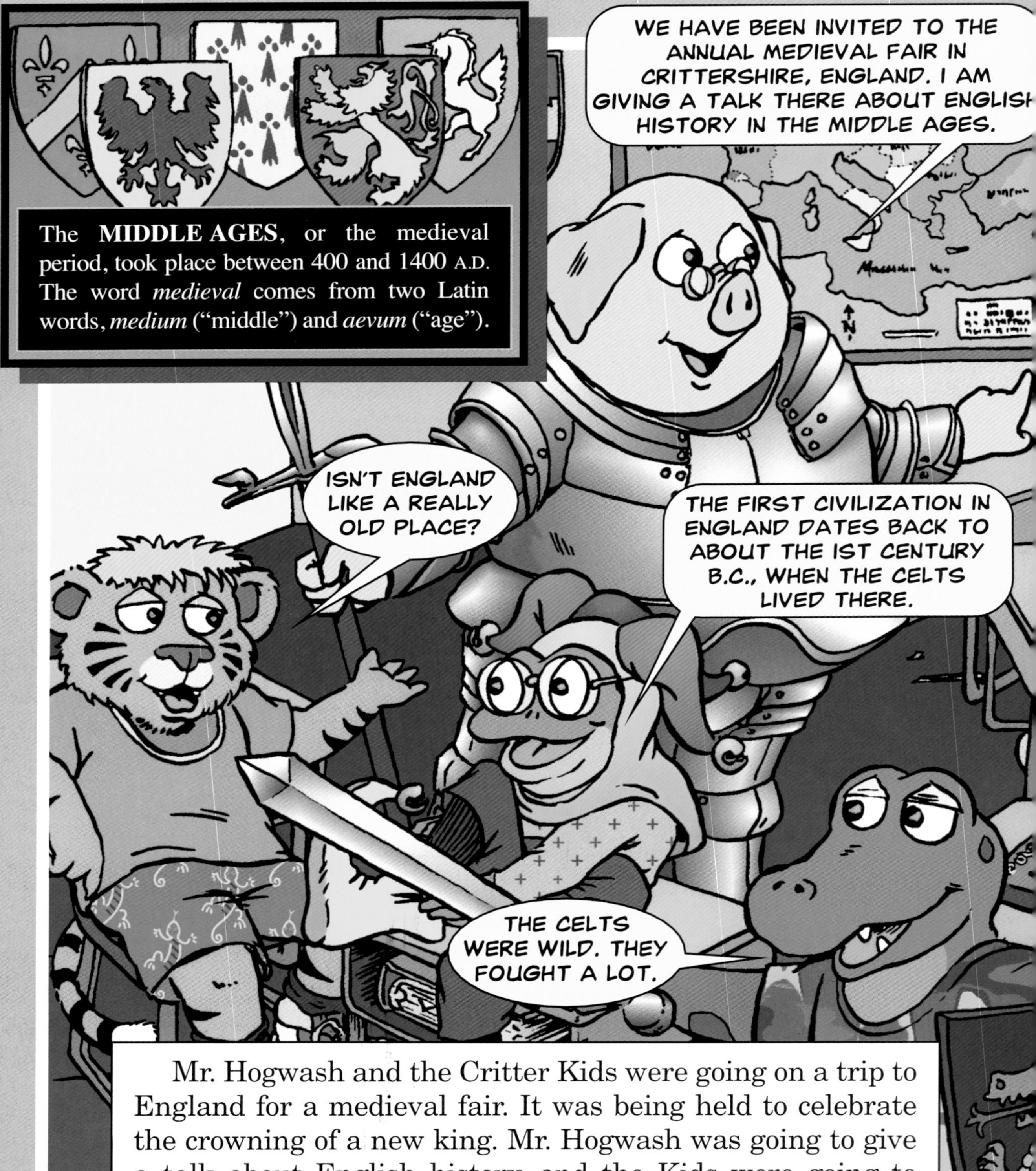
WE HAVE BEEN INVITED TO THE ANNUAL MEDIEVAL FAIR IN CRITTERSHIRE, ENGLAND. I AM GIVING A TALK THERE ABOUT ENGLISH HISTORY IN THE MIDDLE AGES.
ISN'T ENGLAND LIKE A REALLY OLD PLACE?
THE FIRST CIVILIZATION IN ENGLAND DATES BACK TO ABOUT THE 1ST CENTURY B.C., WHEN THE CELTS LIVED THERE.
THE CELTS WERE WILD. THEY FOUGHT A LOT.

Mr. Hogwash and the Critter Kids were going on a trip to England for a medieval fair. It was being held to celebrate the crowning of a new king. Mr. Hogwash was going to give a talk about English history, and the Kids were going to learn all about life in a castle during the Middle Ages.

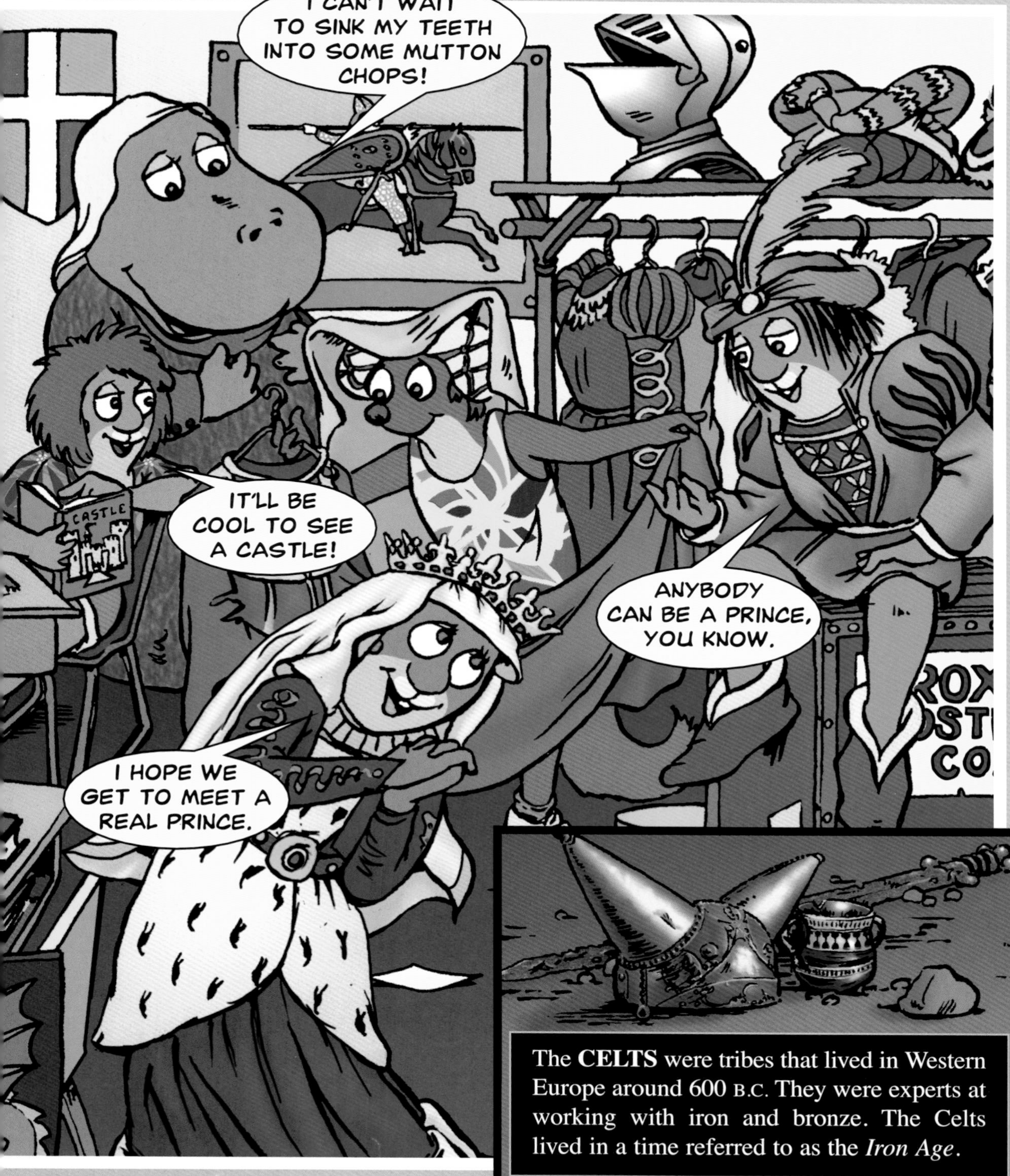
I CAN'T WAIT TO SINK MY TEETH INTO SOME MUTTON CHOPS!
CASTLE
IT'LL BE COOL TO SEE A CASTLE!
I HOPE WE GET TO MEET A REAL PRINCE.
ANYBODY CAN BE A PRINCE, YOU KNOW.

The **CELTS** were tribes that lived in Western Europe around 600 B.C. They were experts at working with iron and bronze. The Celts lived in a time referred to as the *Iron Age*.

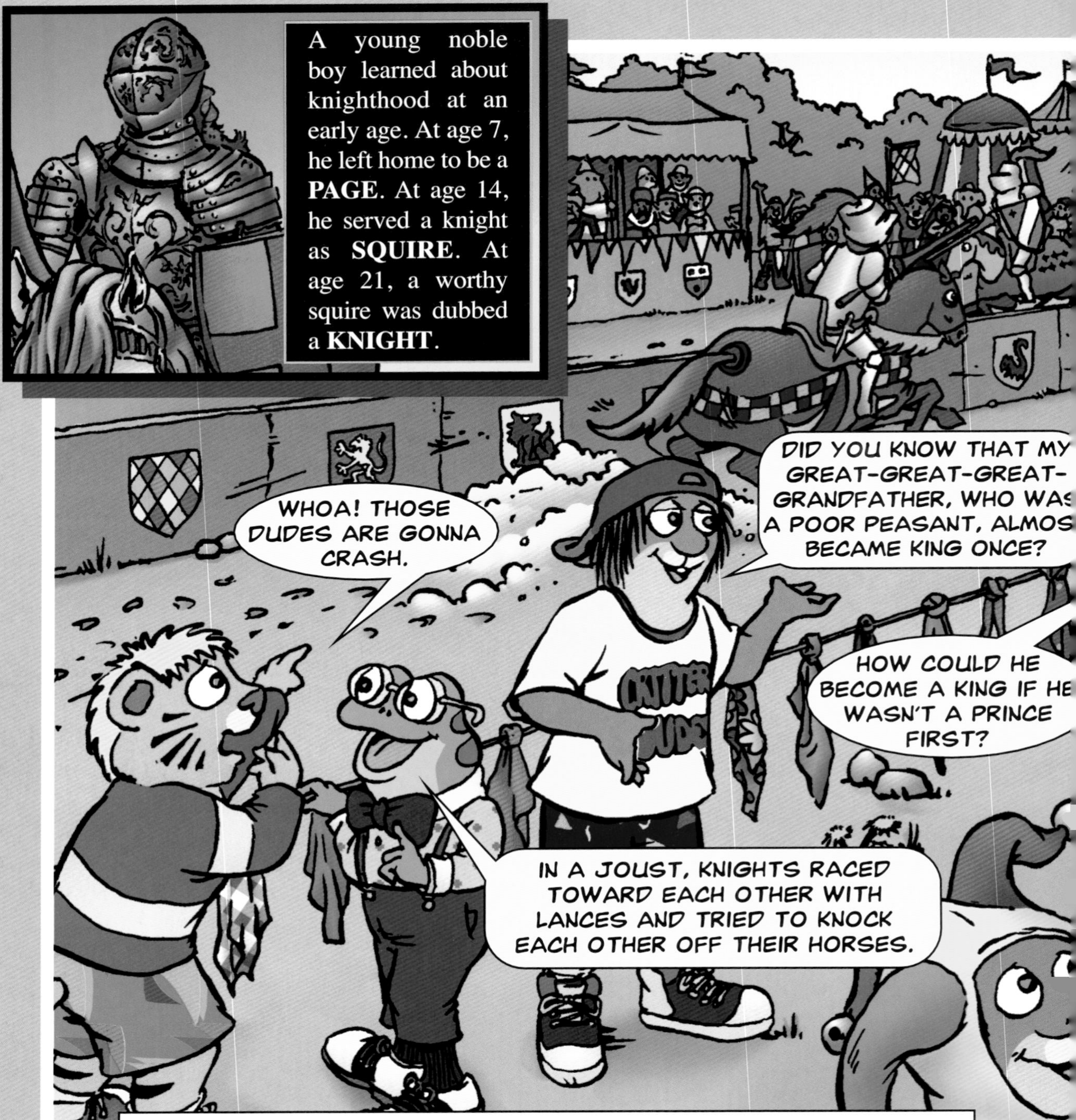
A young noble boy learned about knighthood at an early age. At age 7, he left home to be a **PAGE**. At age 14, he served a knight as **SQUIRE**. At age 21, a worthy squire was dubbed a **KNIGHT**.
WHOA! THOSE DUDES ARE GONNA CRASH.
DID YOU KNOW THAT MY GREAT-GREAT-GREAT-GRANDFATHER, WHO WAS A POOR PEASANT, ALMOS BECAME KING ONCE?
HOW COULD HE BECOME A KING IF HE WASN'T A PRINCE FIRST?
IN A JOUST, KNIGHTS RACED TOWARD EACH OTHER WITH LANCES AND TRIED TO KNOCK EACH OTHER OFF THEIR HORSES.

The next day, Mr. Hogwash and the Critter Kids flew to England. That afternoon, they went to Crittershire for the medieval fair. While Mr. Hogwash gave his talk, LC told the Critter Kids a story.

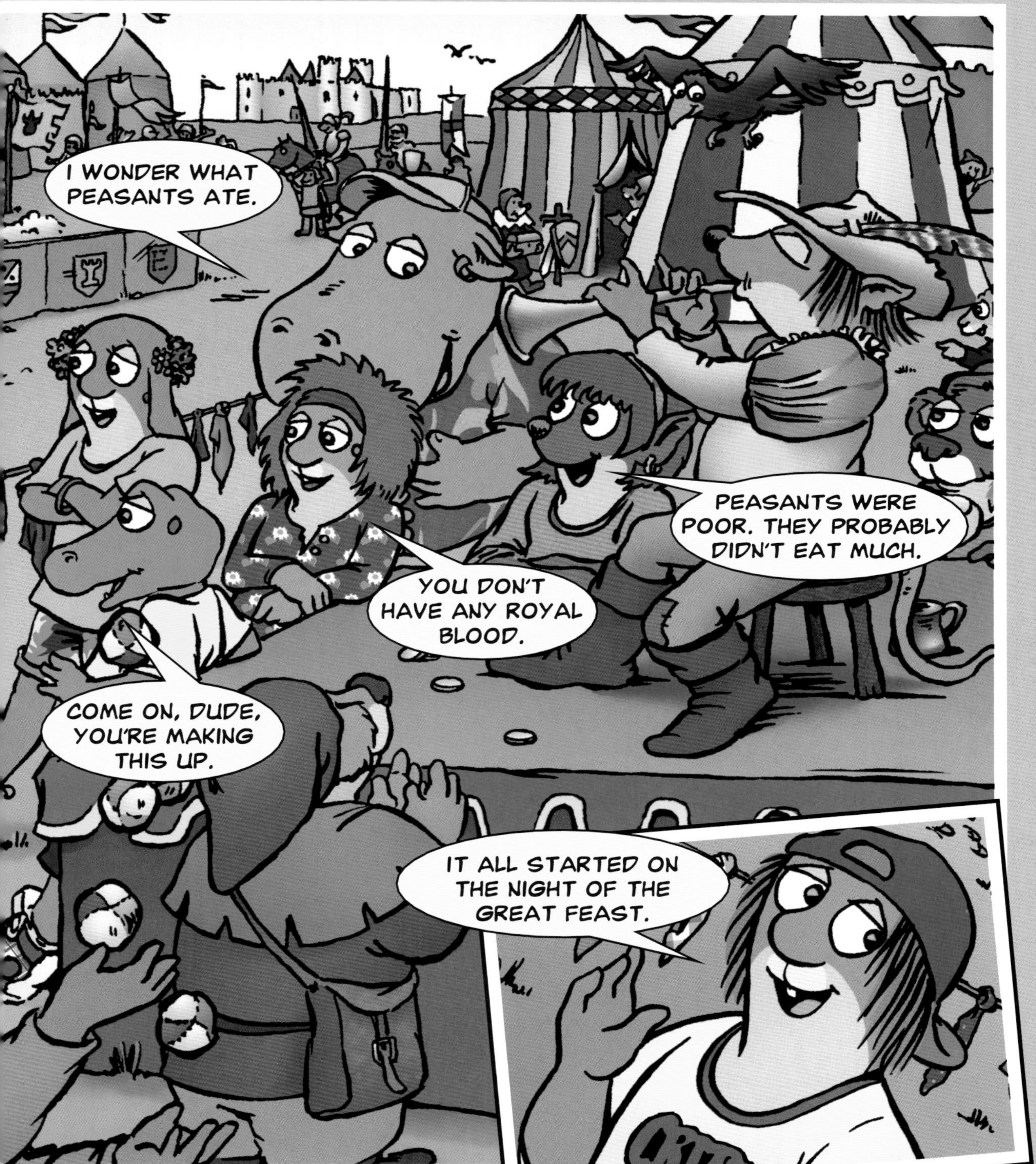
I WONDER WHAT PEASANTS ATE.
PEASANTS WERE POOR. THEY PROBABLY DIDN'T EAT MUCH.
YOU DON'T HAVE ANY ROYAL BLOOD.
COME ON, DUDE, YOU'RE MAKING THIS UP.
IT ALL STARTED ON THE NIGHT OF THE GREAT FEAST.

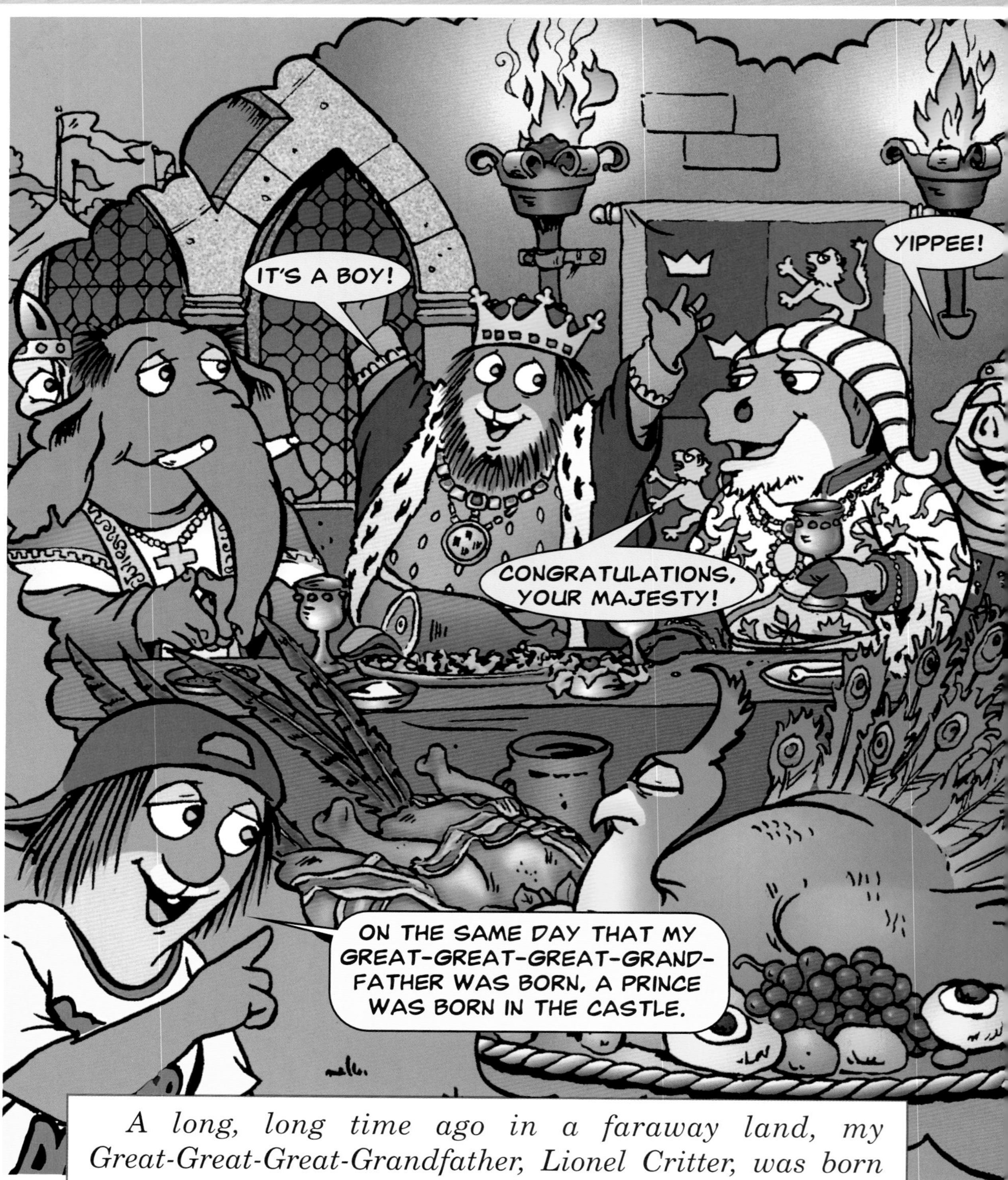
IT'S A BOY!
YIPPEE!
CONGRATULATIONS, YOUR MAJESTY!
ON THE SAME DAY THAT MY GREAT-GREAT-GREAT-GRAND-FATHER WAS BORN, A PRINCE WAS BORN IN THE CASTLE.

A long, long time ago in a faraway land, my Great-Great-Great-Grandfather, Lionel Critter, was born on the same day as the Prince of Crittershire, England.

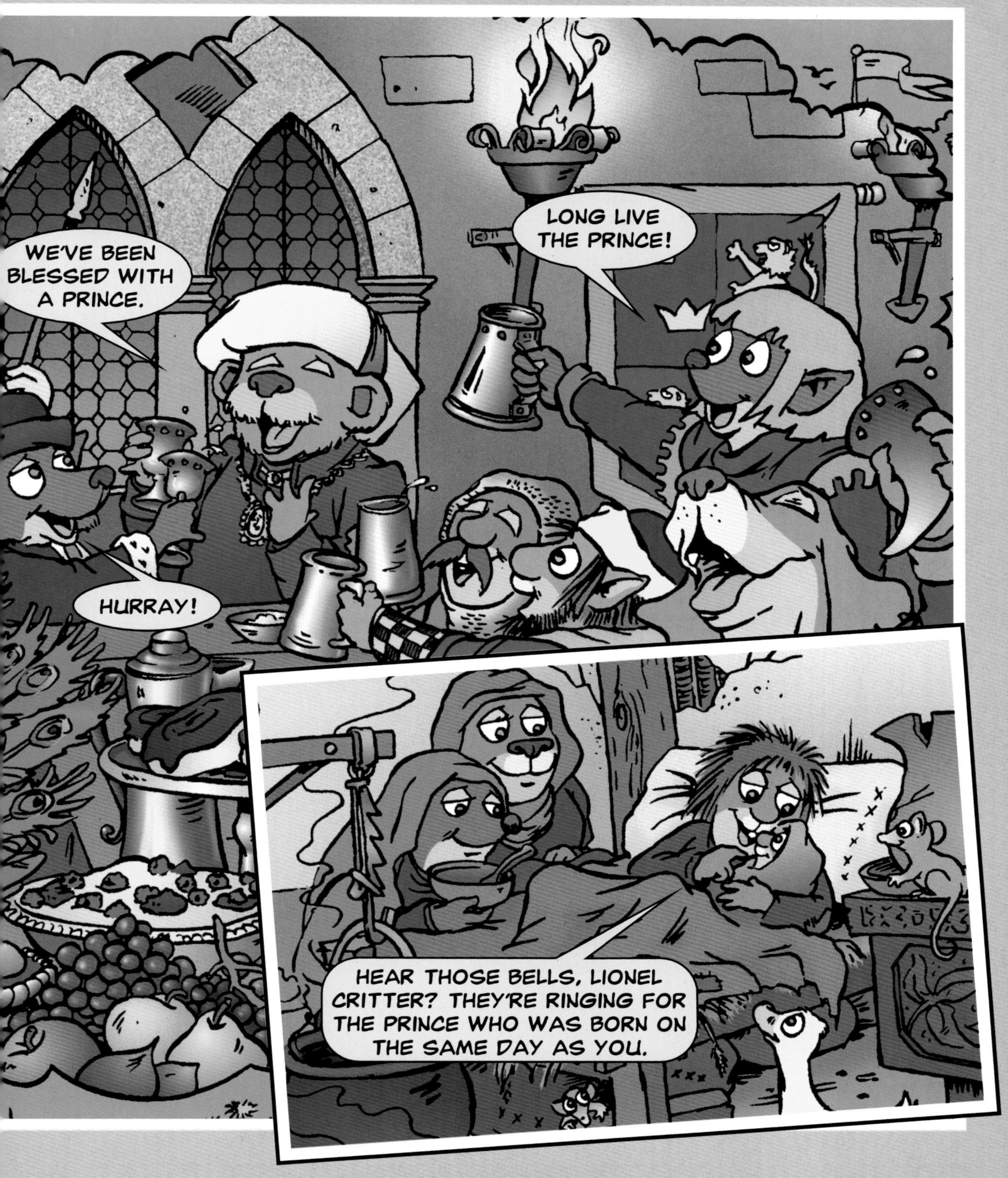
WE'VE BEEN BLESSED WITH A PRINCE.
LONG LIVE THE PRINCE!
HURRAY!
HEAR THOSE BELLS, LIONEL CRITTER? THEY'RE RINGING FOR THE PRINCE WHO WAS BORN ON THE SAME DAY AS YOU.

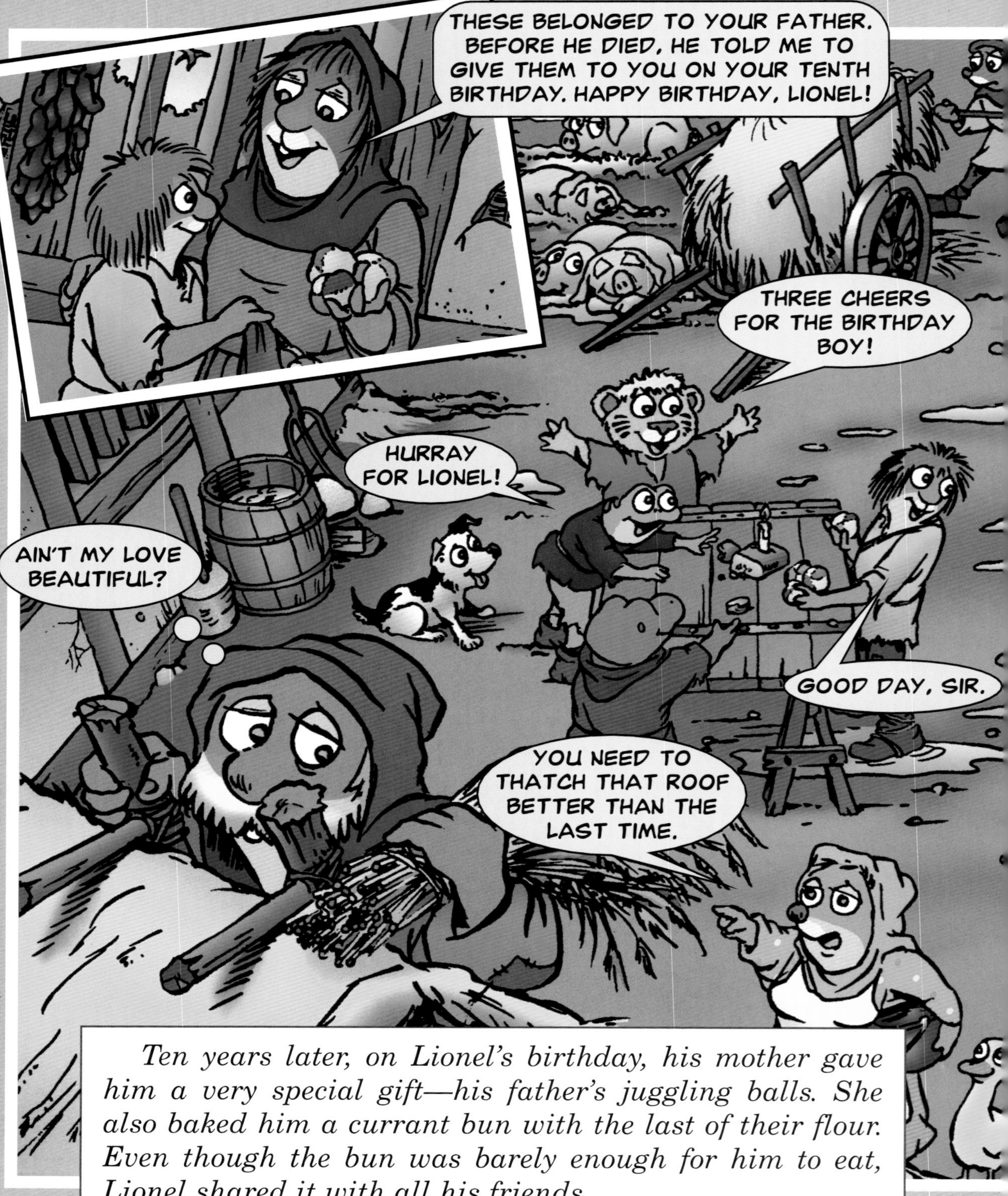
THESE BELONGED TO YOUR FATHER. BEFORE HE DIED, HE TOLD ME TO GIVE THEM TO YOU ON YOUR TENTH BIRTHDAY. HAPPY BIRTHDAY, LIONEL!
THREE CHEERS FOR THE BIRTHDAY BOY!
HURRAY FOR LIONEL!
AIN'T MY LOVE BEAUTIFUL?
GOOD DAY, SIR.
YOU NEED TO THATCH THAT ROOF BETTER THAN THE LAST TIME.

Ten years later, on Lionel's birthday, his mother gave him a very special gift—his father's juggling balls. She also baked him a currant bun with the last of their flour. Even though the bun was barely enough for him to eat, Lionel shared it with all his friends.

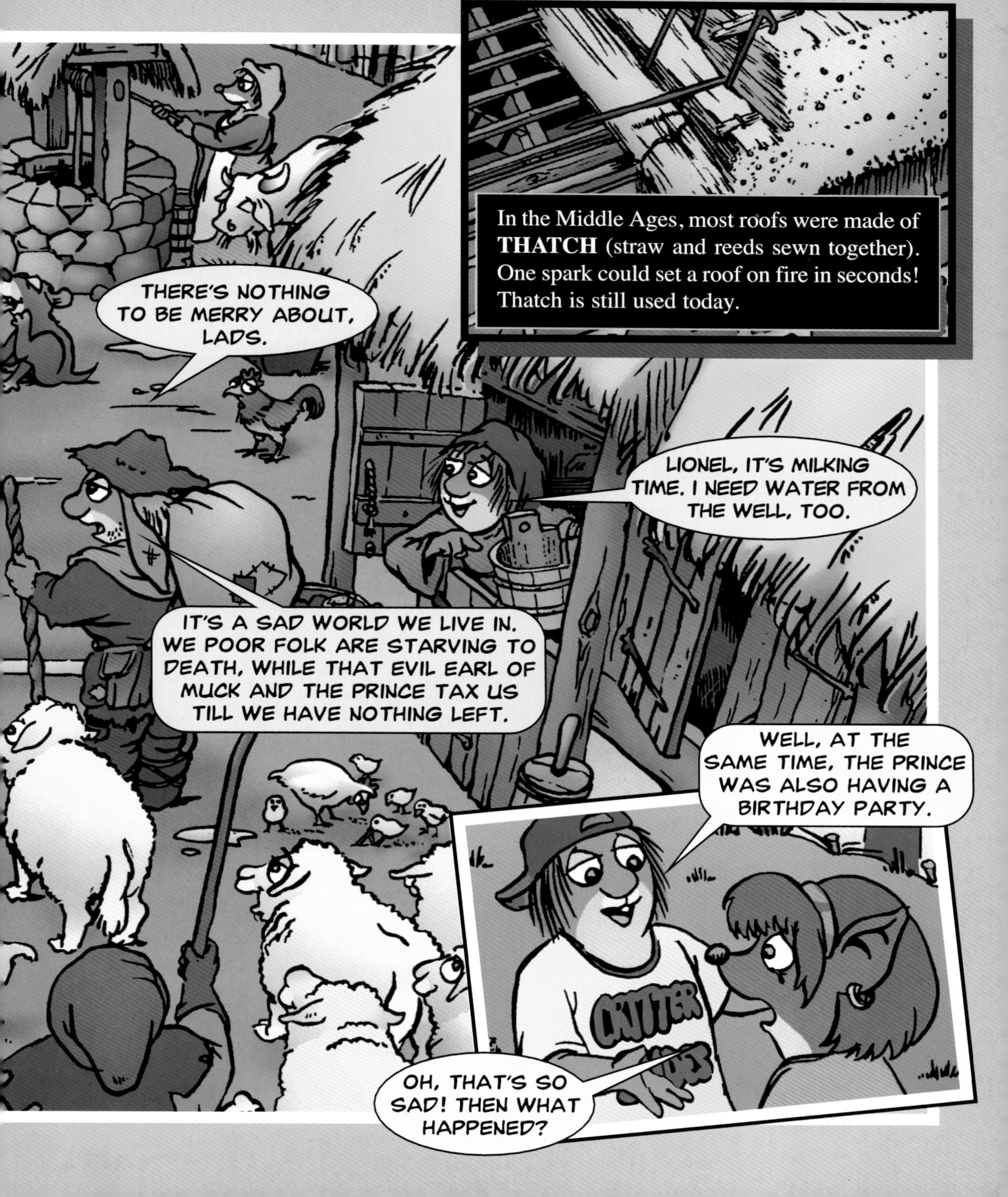
In the Middle Ages, most roofs were made of THATCH (straw and reeds sewn together). One spark could set a roof on fire in seconds! Thatch is still used today.
THERE'S NOTHING TO BE MERRY ABOUT, LADS.
LIONEL, IT'S MILKING TIME. I NEED WATER FROM THE WELL, TOO.
IT'S A SAD WORLD WE LIVE IN. WE POOR FOLK ARE STARVING TO DEATH, WHILE THAT EVIL EARL OF MUCK AND THE PRINCE TAX US TILL WE HAVE NOTHING LEFT.
WELL, AT THE SAME TIME, THE PRINCE WAS ALSO HAVING A BIRTHDAY PARTY.
OH, THAT'S SO SAD! THEN WHAT HAPPENED?
CRITTER

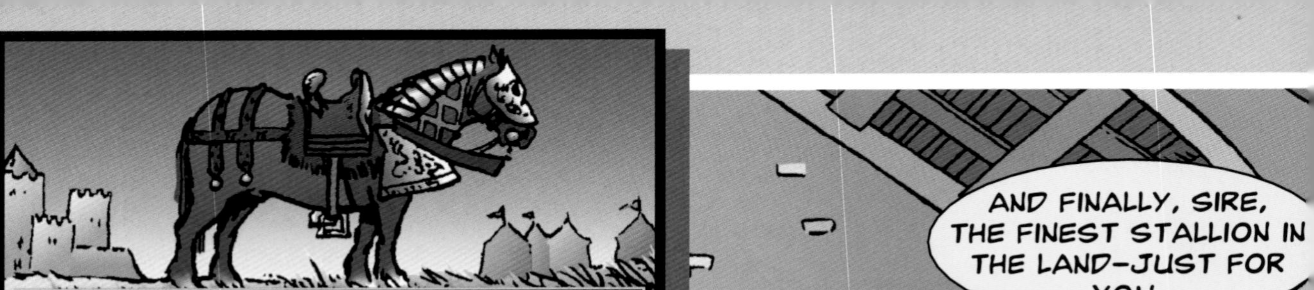

HORSES were prized by knights—especially stallions. Knights spent as much money caring for their horses as they could afford. They often shared their tents with them.

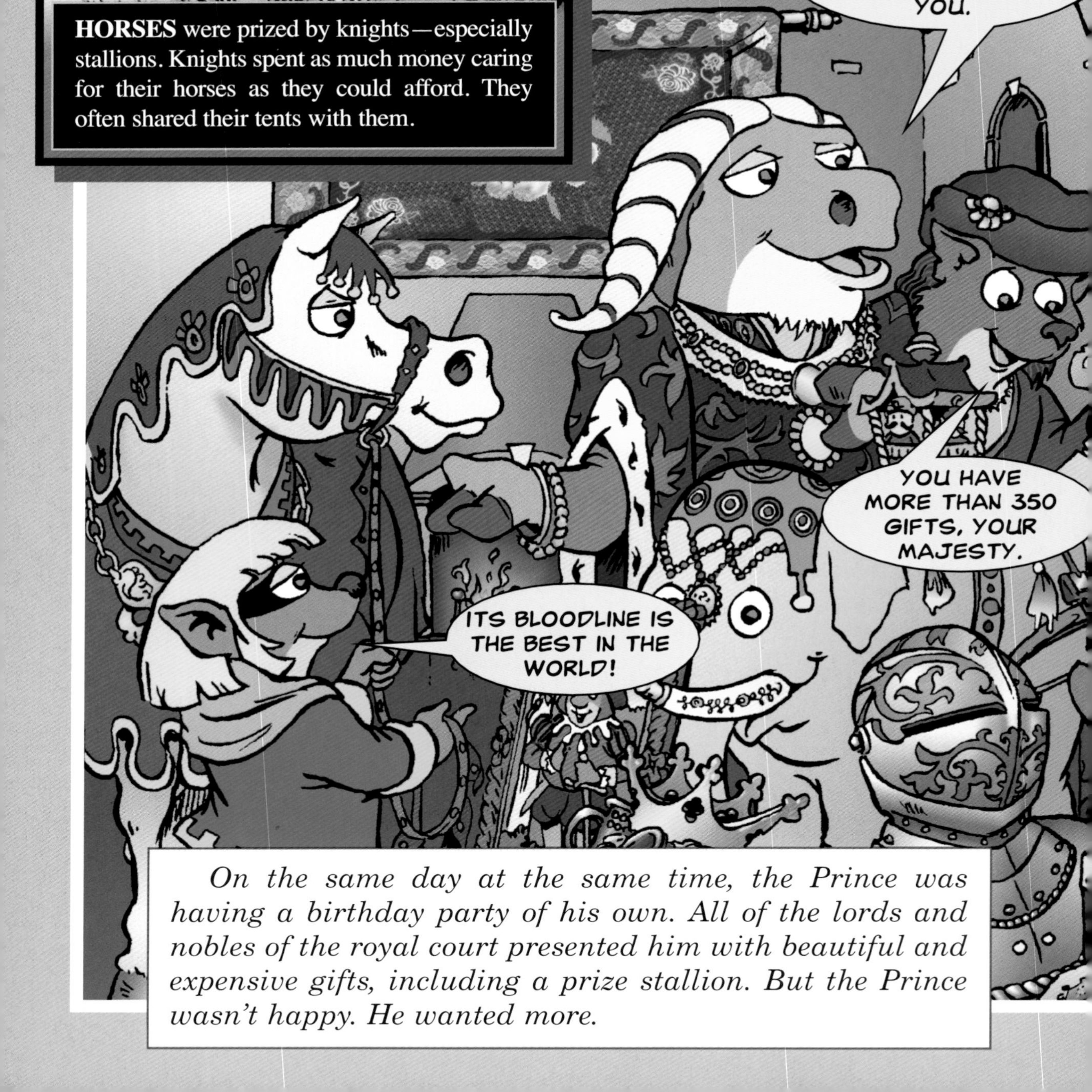
AND FINALLY, SIRE, THE FINEST STALLION IN THE LAND–JUST FOR YOU.
YOU HAVE MORE THAN 350 GIFTS, YOUR MAJESTY.
ITS BLOODLINE IS THE BEST IN THE WORLD!

On the same day at the same time, the Prince was having a birthday party of his own. All of the lords and nobles of the royal court presented him with beautiful and expensive gifts, including a prize stallion. But the Prince wasn't happy. He wanted more.

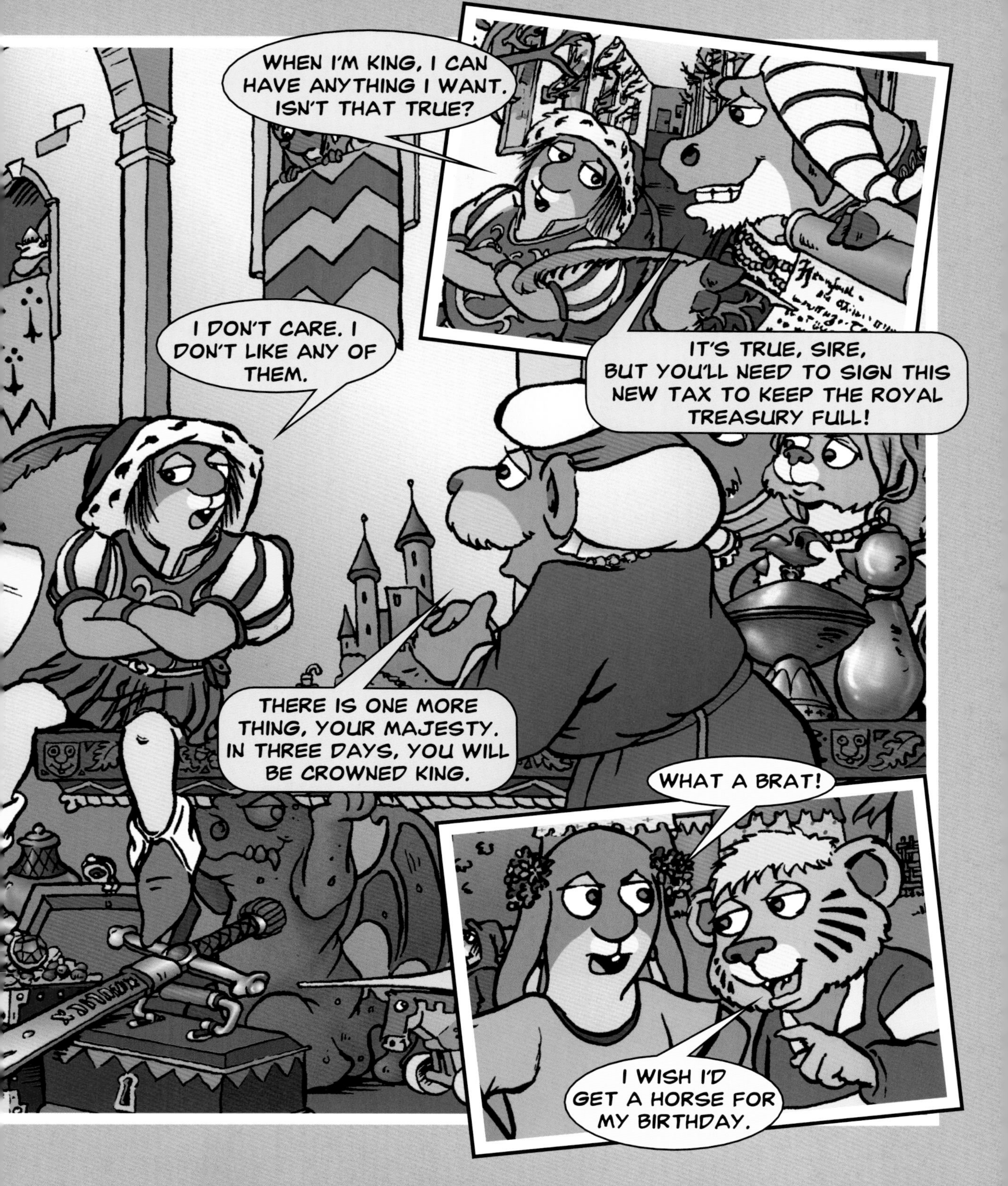
WHEN I'M KING, I CAN HAVE ANYTHING I WANT. ISN'T THAT TRUE?
IT'S TRUE, SIRE, BUT YOU'LL NEED TO SIGN THIS NEW TAX TO KEEP THE ROYAL TREASURY FULL!
I DON'T CARE. I DON'T LIKE ANY OF THEM.
THERE IS ONE MORE THING, YOUR MAJESTY. IN THREE DAYS, YOU WILL BE CROWNED KING.
WHAT A BRAT!
I WISH I'D GET A HORSE FOR MY BIRTHDAY.

FALCONRY was a popular sport during the Middle Ages. Also known as *birds of the fist*, falcons were valued by their owners. Some even took their birds into church.

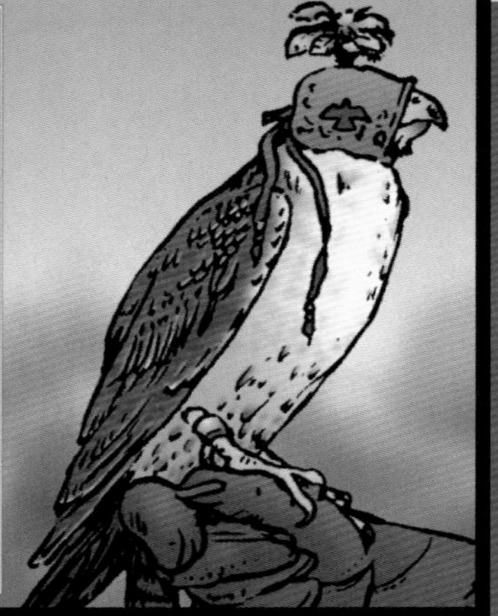

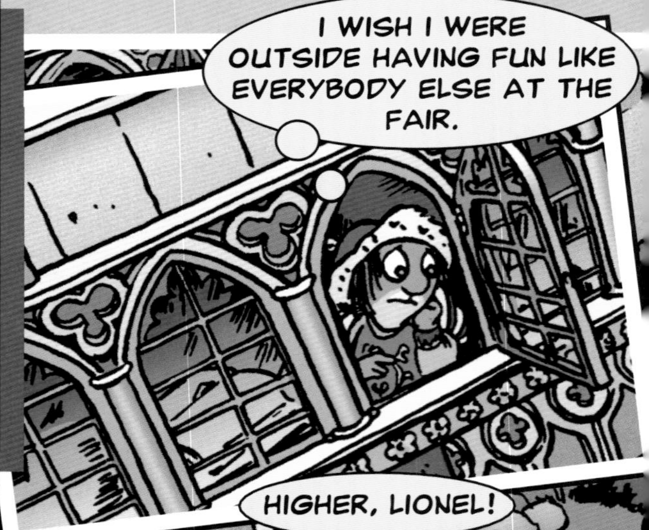
I WISH I WERE OUTSIDE HAVING FUN LIKE EVERYBODY ELSE AT THE FAIR.

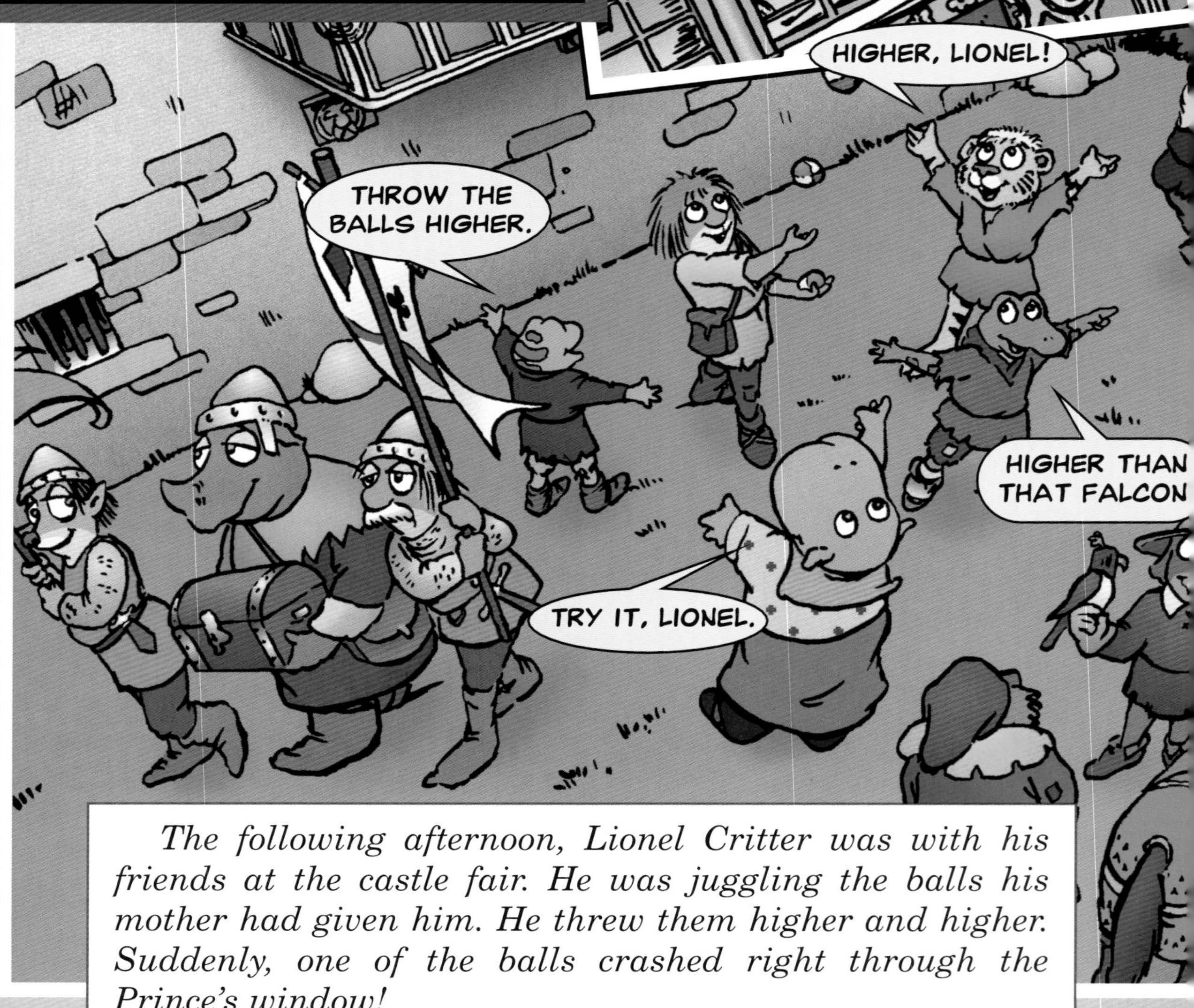
HIGHER, LIONEL!
THROW THE BALLS HIGHER.
HIGHER THAN THAT FALCON
TRY IT, LIONEL.

The following afternoon, Lionel Critter was with his friends at the castle fair. He was juggling the balls his mother had given him. He threw them higher and higher. Suddenly, one of the balls crashed right through the Prince's window!

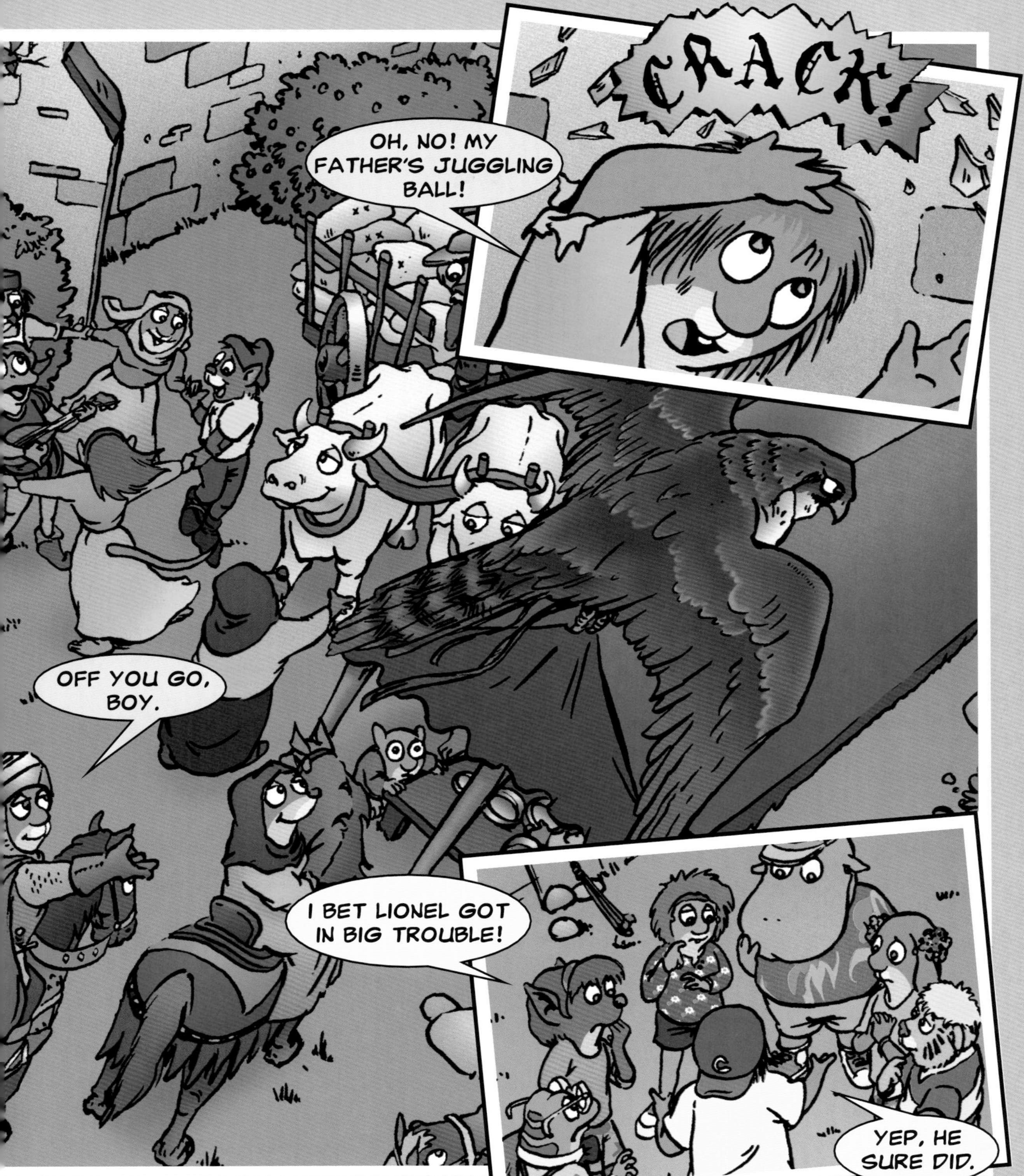
CRACK!
OH, NO! MY FATHER'S JUGGLING BALL!
OFF YOU GO, BOY.
I BET LIONEL GOT IN BIG TROUBLE!
YEP, HE SURE DID.

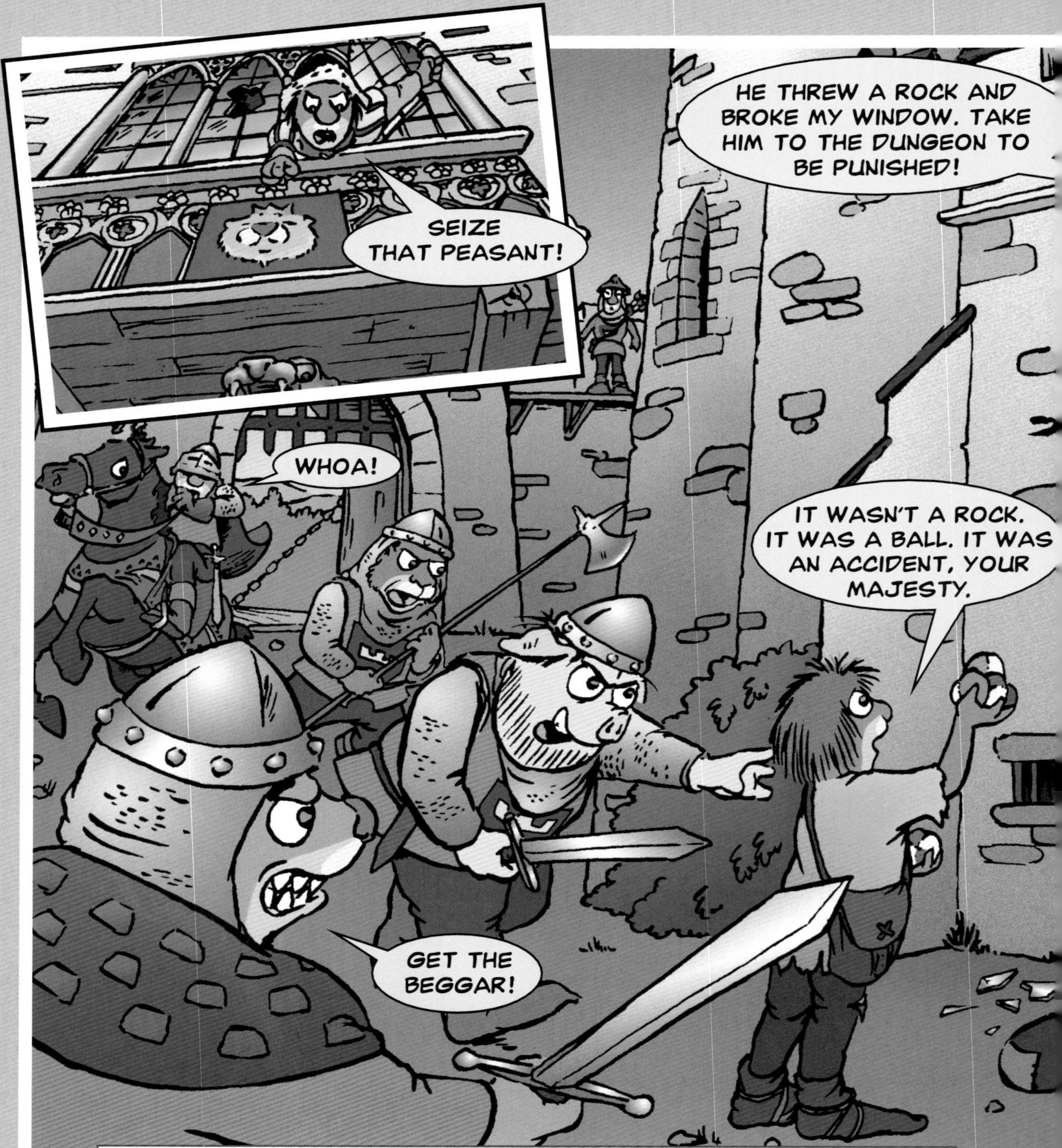
SEIZE THAT PEASANT!
HE THREW A ROCK AND BROKE MY WINDOW. TAKE HIM TO THE DUNGEON TO BE PUNISHED!
WHOA!
IT WASN'T A ROCK. IT WAS A BALL. IT WAS AN ACCIDENT, YOUR MAJESTY.
GET THE BEGGAR!

The Prince was very angry. He commanded the castle guards to lock Lionel in the dungeon and have him punished.

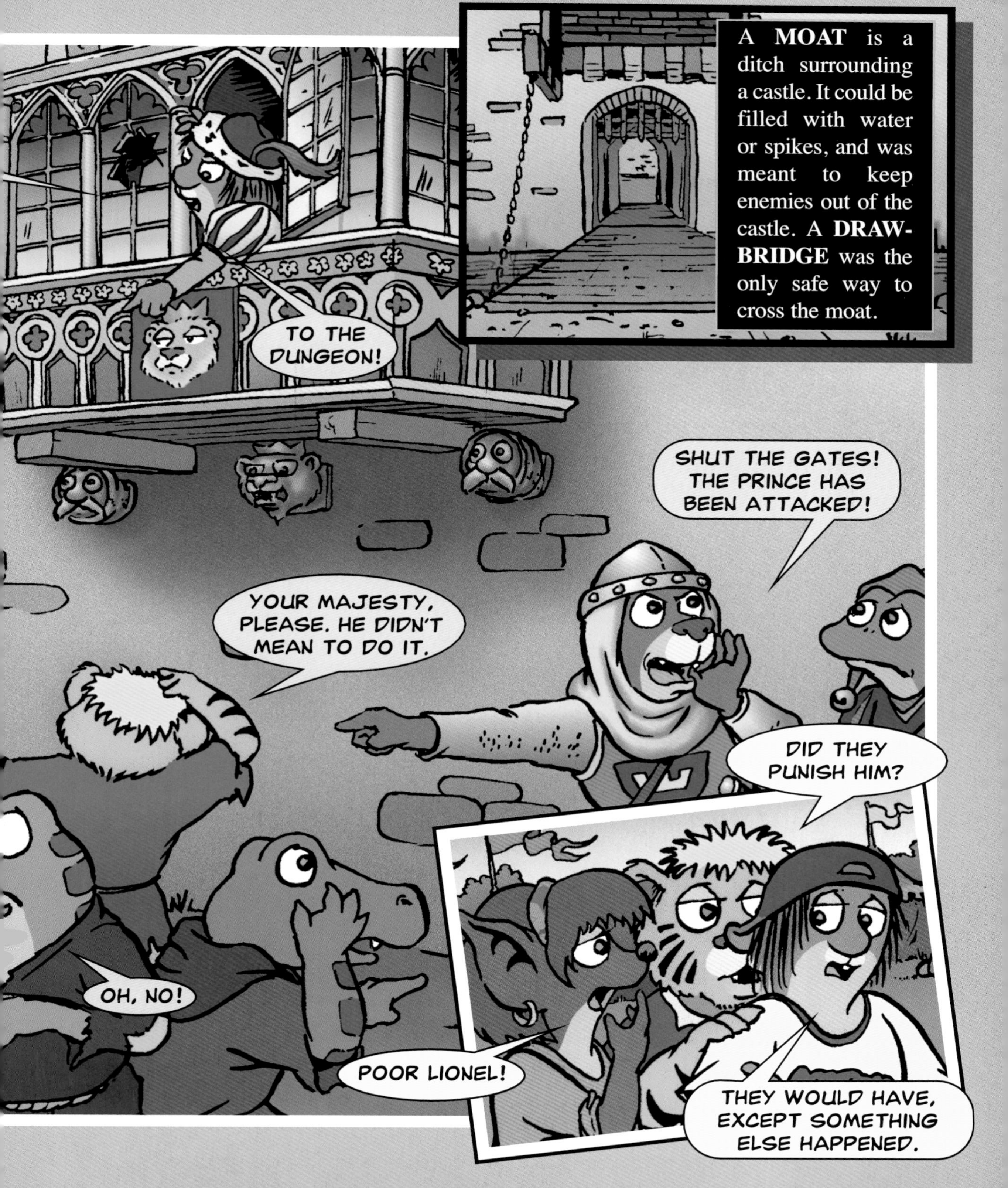

TO THE DUNGEON!
A **MOAT** is a ditch surrounding a castle. It could be filled with water or spikes, and was meant to keep enemies out of the castle. A **DRAW-BRIDGE** was the only safe way to cross the moat.
SHUT THE GATES! THE PRINCE HAS BEEN ATTACKED!
YOUR MAJESTY, PLEASE. HE DIDN'T MEAN TO DO IT.
OH, NO!
POOR LIONEL!
DID THEY PUNISH HIM?
THEY WOULD HAVE, EXCEPT SOMETHING ELSE HAPPENED.

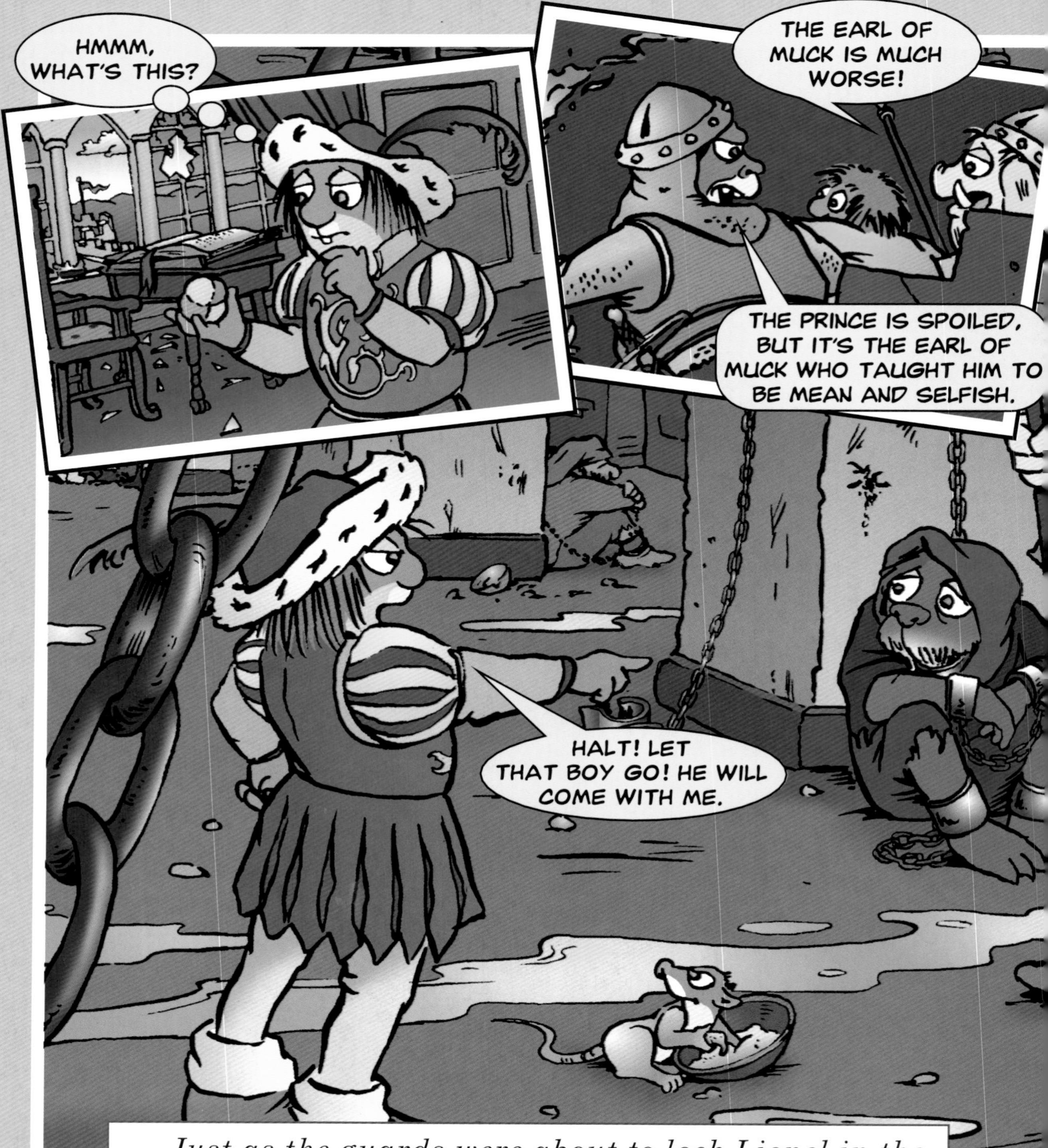
HMMM, WHAT'S THIS?
THE EARL OF MUCK IS MUCH WORSE!
THE PRINCE IS SPOILED, BUT IT'S THE EARL OF MUCK WHO TAUGHT HIM TO BE MEAN AND SELFISH.
HALT! LET THAT BOY GO! HE WILL COME WITH ME.

Just as the guards were about to lock Lionel in the dungeon, the Prince suddenly appeared. He told the guards that he would take care of Lionel himself.

DUNGEONS were damp, dirty spaces where prisoners of a castle were kept and punished. Some were chained to walls by their hands and feet, and by their necks with an iron collar weighing up to 35 pounds.

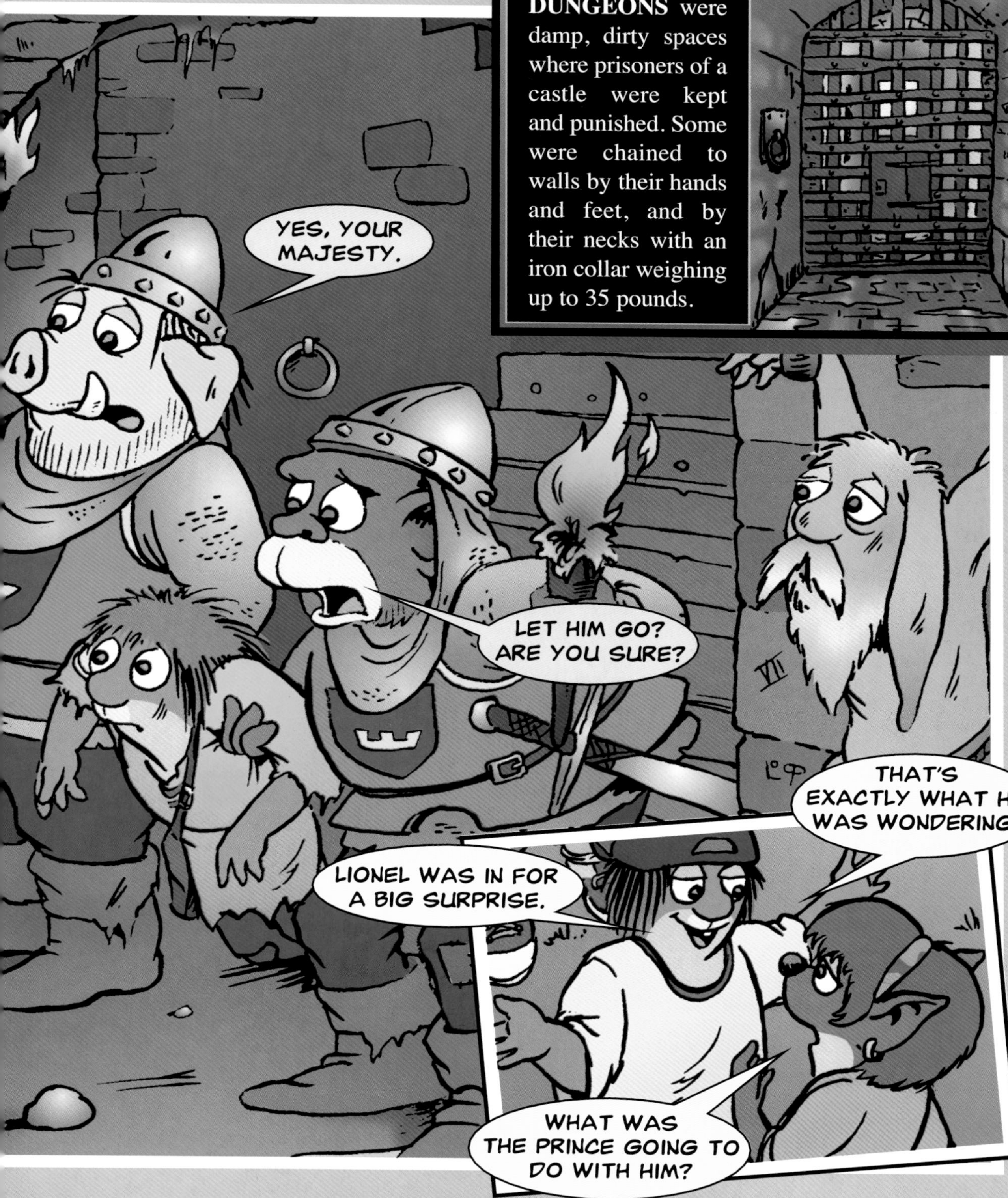
YES, YOUR MAJESTY.
LET HIM GO? ARE YOU SURE?
LIONEL WAS IN FOR A BIG SURPRISE.
THAT'S EXACTLY WHAT HE WAS WONDERING.
WHAT WAS THE PRINCE GOING TO DO WITH HIM?

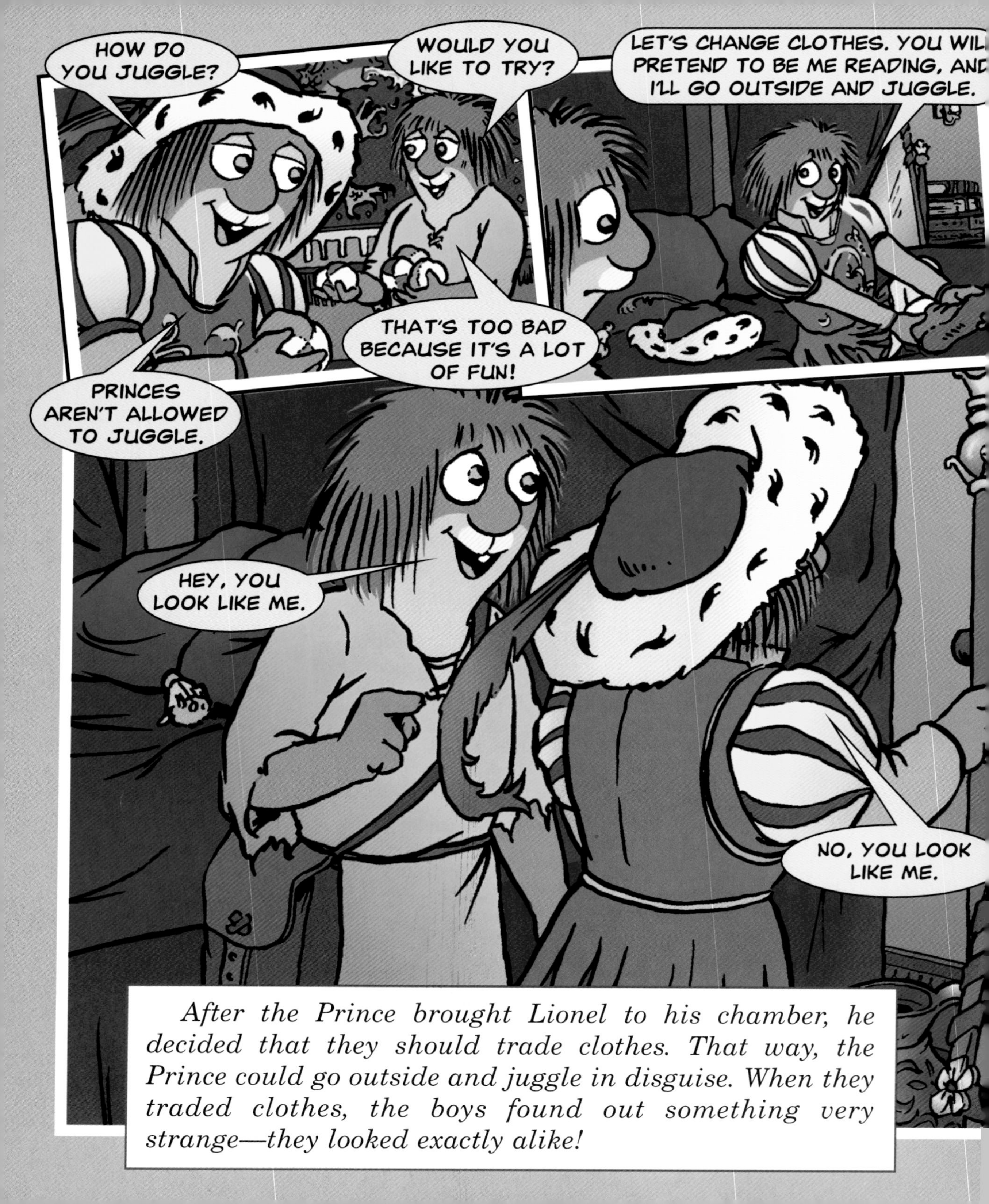
HOW DO YOU JUGGLE?
PRINCES AREN'T ALLOWED TO JUGGLE.
WOULD YOU LIKE TO TRY?
THAT'S TOO BAD BECAUSE IT'S A LOT OF FUN!
LET'S CHANGE CLOTHES. YOU WIL
PRETEND TO BE ME READING, AN
I'LL GO OUTSIDE AND JUGGLE.
HEY, YOU LOOK LIKE ME.
NO, YOU LOOK LIKE ME.

After the Prince brought Lionel to his chamber, he decided that they should trade clothes. That way, the Prince could go outside and juggle in disguise. When they traded clothes, the boys found out something very strange—they looked exactly alike!

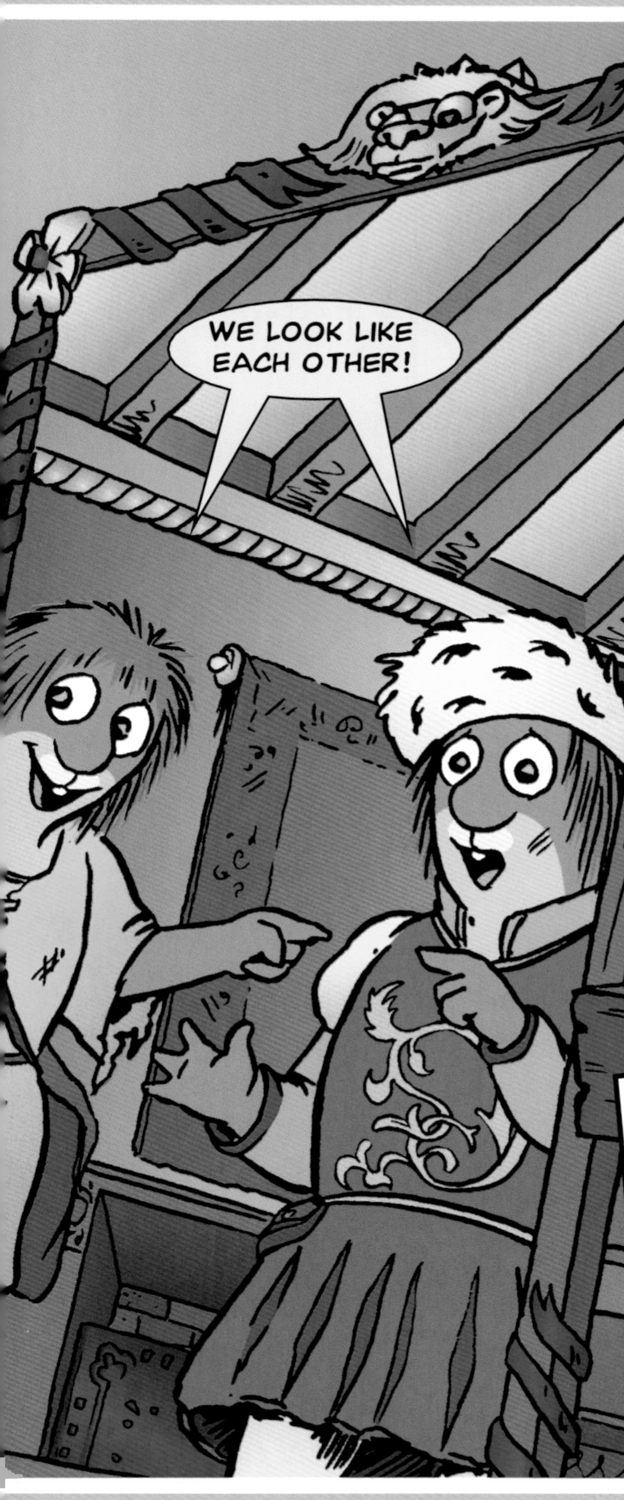
WE LOOK LIKE EACH OTHER!

ILLUMINATED MANUSCRIPTS were books painted in bright colors, gold, and silver. Their covers were often decorated with gems. Because there were no printing presses, books were copied by hand.

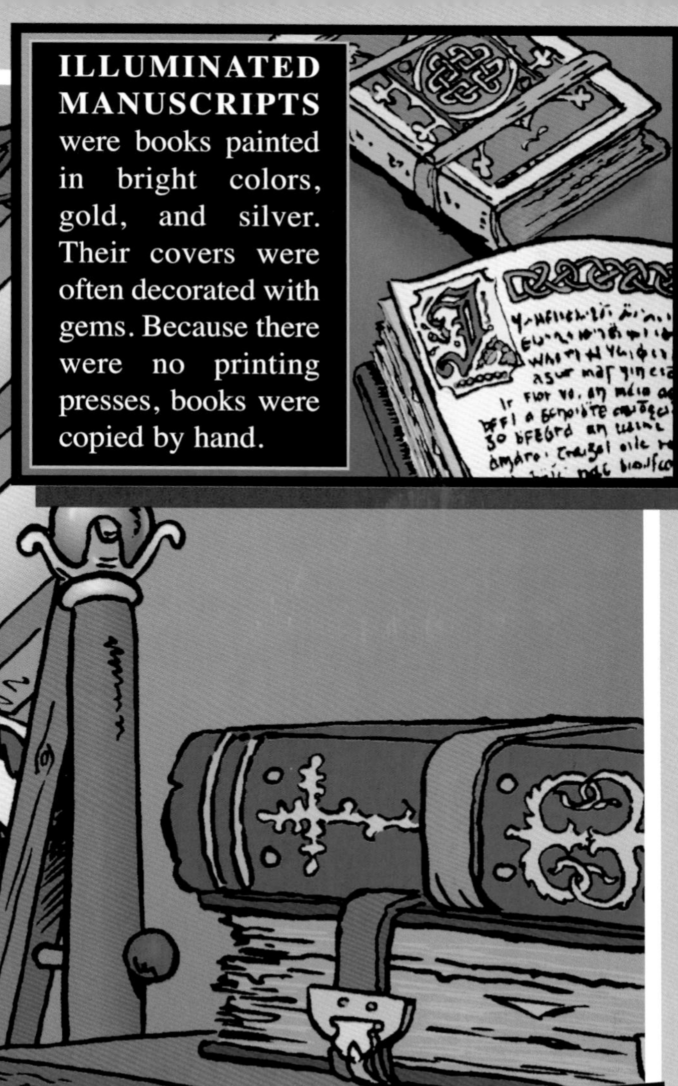

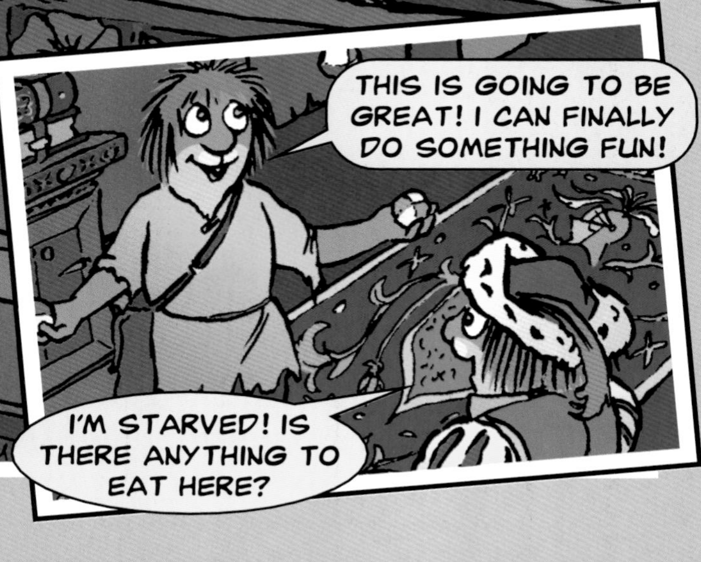
THIS IS GOING TO BE GREAT! I CAN FINALLY DO SOMETHING FUN!
I'M STARVED! IS THERE ANYTHING TO EAT HERE?

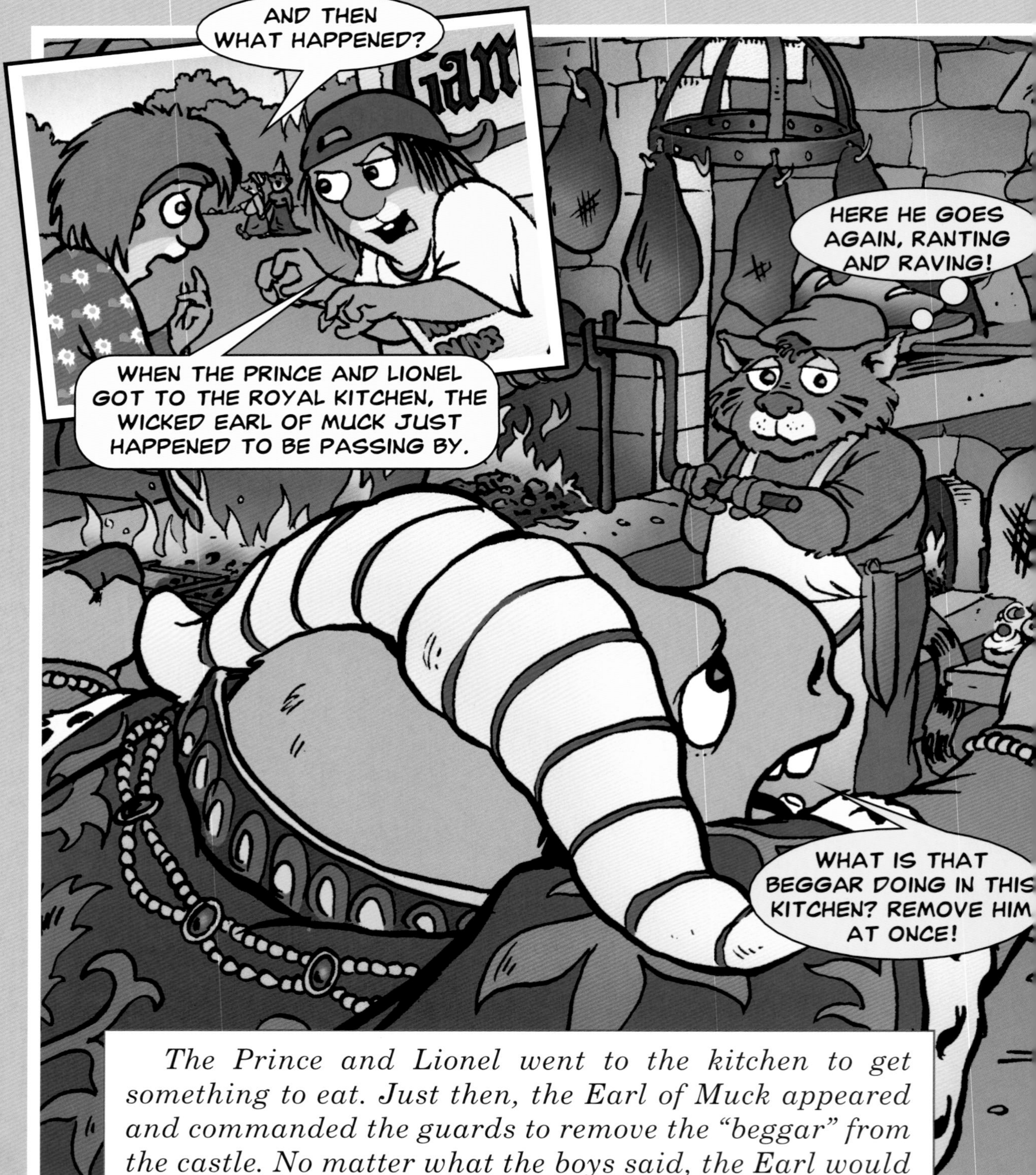
AND THEN WHAT HAPPENED?
WHEN THE PRINCE AND LIONEL GOT TO THE ROYAL KITCHEN, THE WICKED EARL OF MUCK JUST HAPPENED TO BE PASSING BY.
HERE HE GOES AGAIN, RANTING AND RAVING!
WHAT IS THAT BEGGAR DOING IN THIS KITCHEN? REMOVE HIM AT ONCE!

The Prince and Lionel went to the kitchen to get something to eat. Just then, the Earl of Muck appeared and commanded the guards to remove the "beggar" from the castle. No matter what the boys said, the Earl would not listen. So, the Prince was mistakenly taken away.

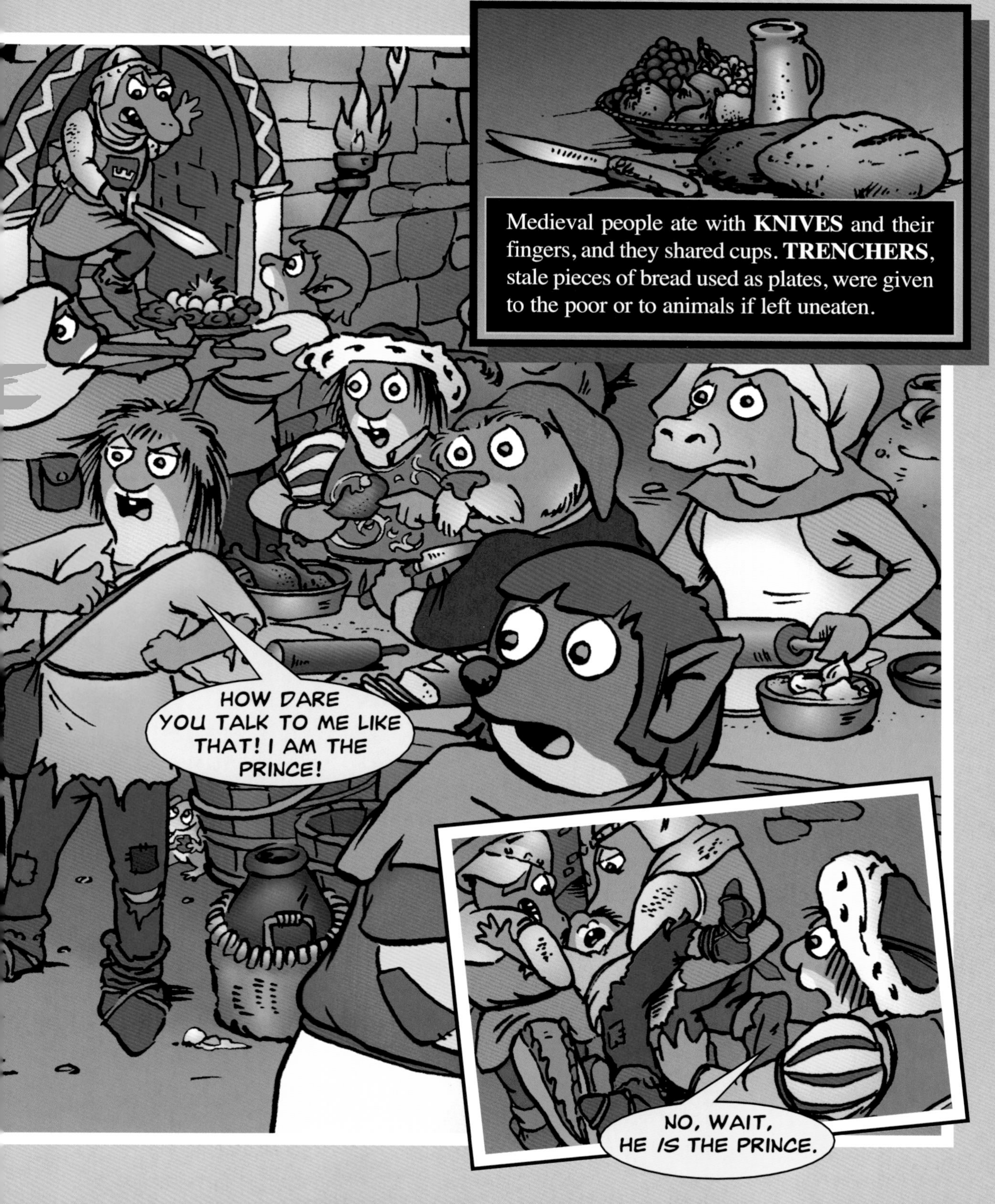
Medieval people ate with **KNIVES** and their fingers, and they shared cups. **TRENCHERS**, stale pieces of bread used as plates, were given to the poor or to animals if left uneaten.
HOW DARE YOU TALK TO ME LIKE THAT! I AM THE PRINCE!
NO, WAIT, HE *IS* THE PRINCE.

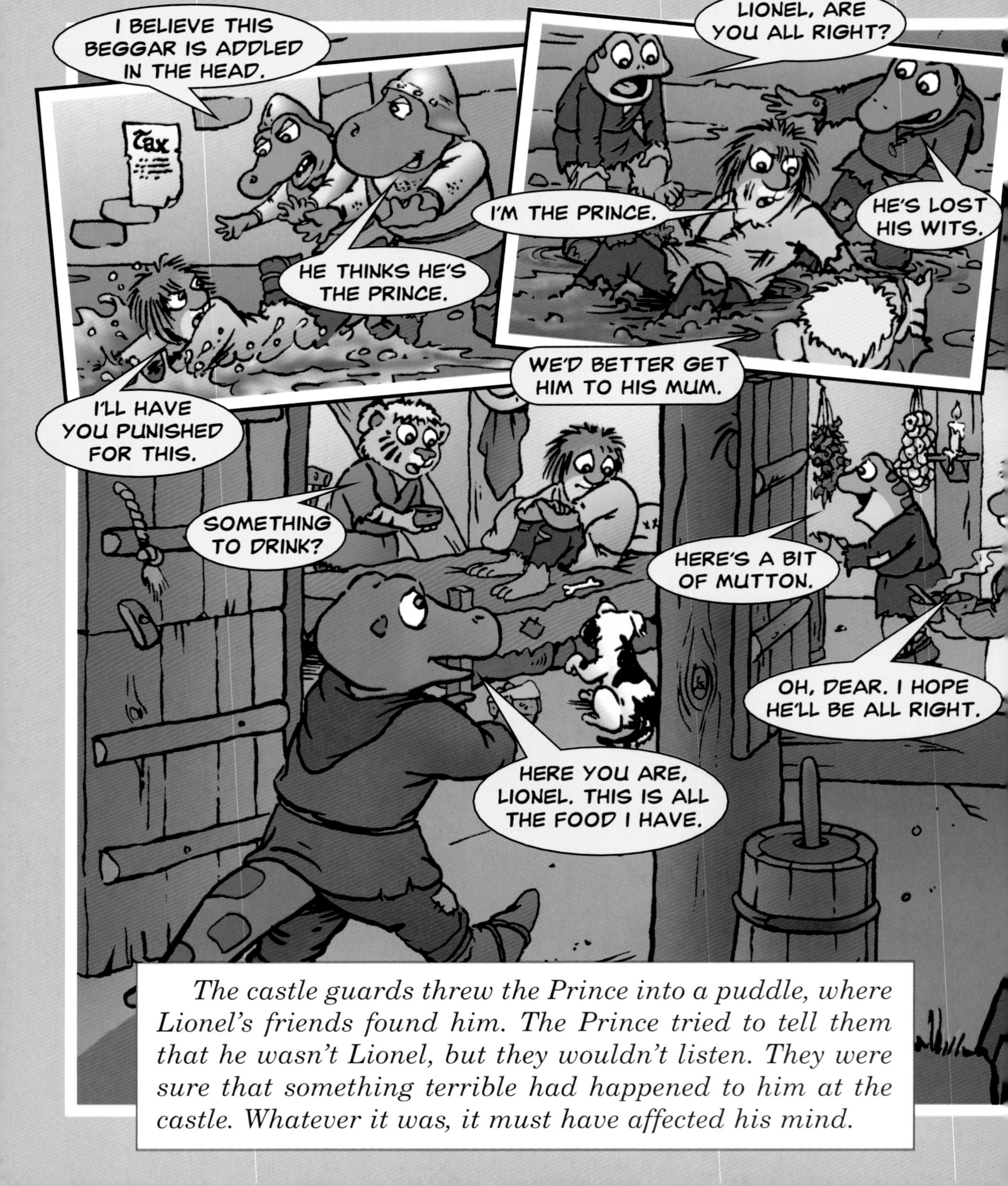
I BELIEVE THIS BEGGAR IS ADDLED IN THE HEAD.
Tax
HE THINKS HE'S THE PRINCE.
I'LL HAVE YOU PUNISHED FOR THIS.
LIONEL, ARE YOU ALL RIGHT?
I'M THE PRINCE.
HE'S LOST HIS WITS.
WE'D BETTER GET HIM TO HIS MUM.
SOMETHING TO DRINK?
HERE'S A BIT OF MUTTON.
OH, DEAR. I HOPE HE'LL BE ALL RIGHT.
HERE YOU ARE, LIONEL. THIS IS ALL THE FOOD I HAVE.

The castle guards threw the Prince into a puddle, where Lionel's friends found him. The Prince tried to tell them that he wasn't Lionel, but they wouldn't listen. They were sure that something terrible had happened to him at the castle. Whatever it was, it must have affected his mind.

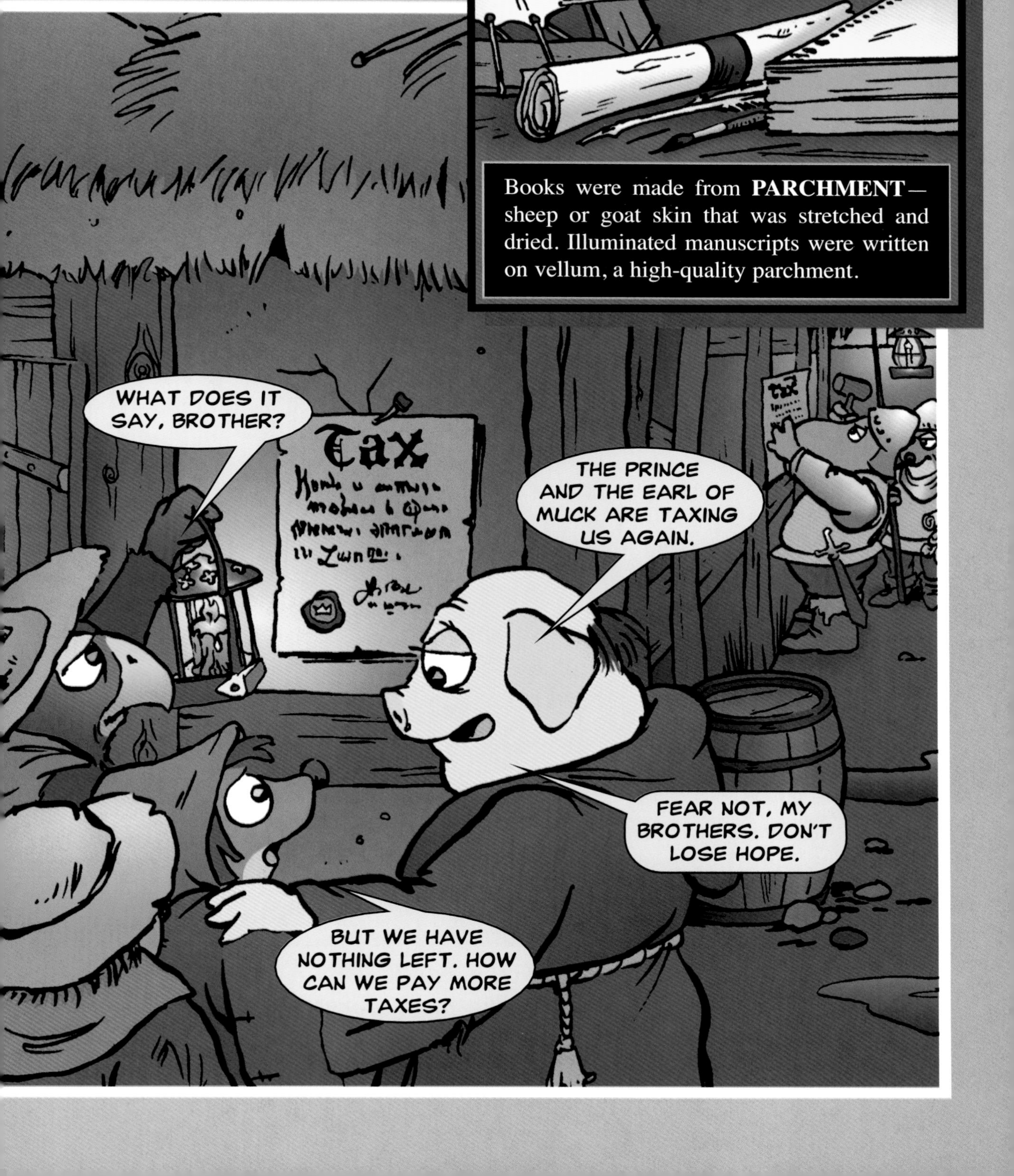
Tax
WHAT DOES IT SAY, BROTHER?
THE PRINCE AND THE EARL OF MUCK ARE TAXING US AGAIN.
FEAR NOT, MY BROTHERS. DON'T LOSE HOPE.
BUT WE HAVE NOTHING LEFT. HOW CAN WE PAY MORE TAXES?

Books were made from **PARCHMENT**—sheep or goat skin that was stretched and dried. Illuminated manuscripts were written on vellum, a high-quality parchment.

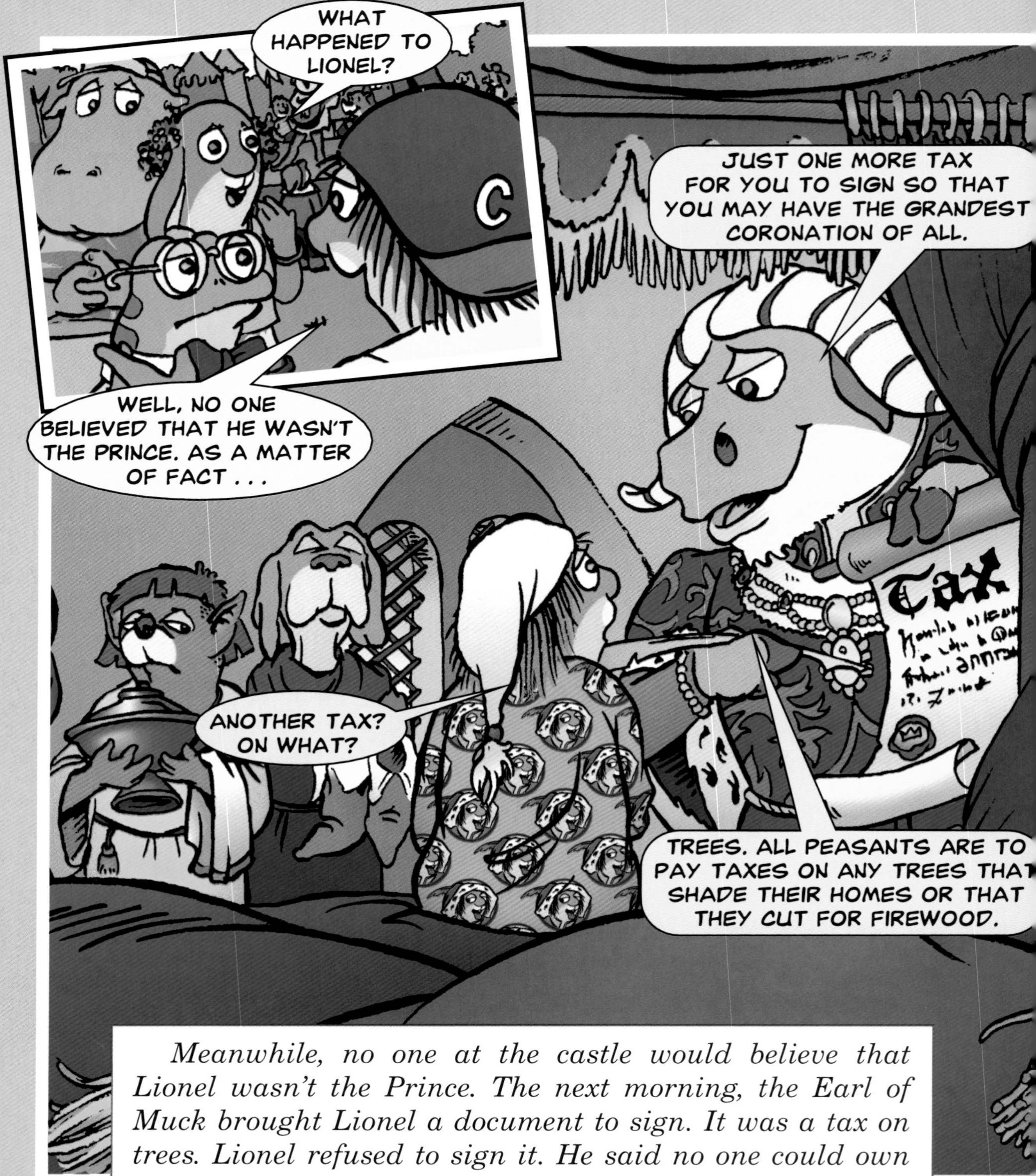
WHAT HAPPENED TO LIONEL?
WELL, NO ONE BELIEVED THAT HE WASN'T THE PRINCE. AS A MATTER OF FACT . . .
JUST ONE MORE TAX FOR YOU TO SIGN SO THAT YOU MAY HAVE THE GRANDEST CORONATION OF ALL.
Tax
ANOTHER TAX? ON WHAT?
TREES. ALL PEASANTS ARE TO PAY TAXES ON ANY TREES THAT SHADE THEIR HOMES OR THAT THEY CUT FOR FIREWOOD.

Meanwhile, no one at the castle would believe that Lionel wasn't the Prince. The next morning, the Earl of Muck brought Lionel a document to sign. It was a tax on trees. Lionel refused to sign it. He said no one could own trees—not even a king.

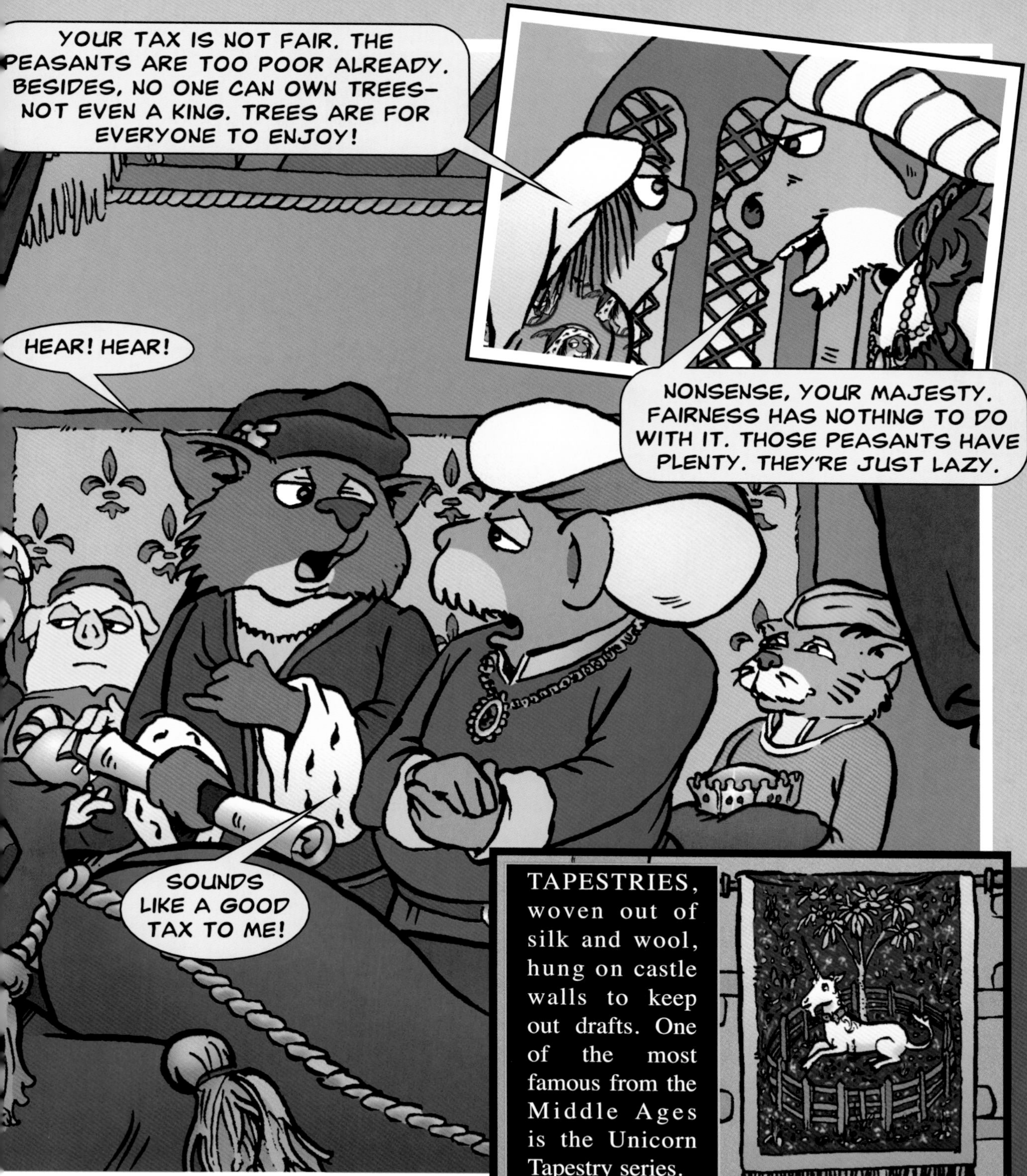
YOUR TAX IS NOT FAIR. THE PEASANTS ARE TOO POOR ALREADY. BESIDES, NO ONE CAN OWN TREES— NOT EVEN A KING. TREES ARE FOR EVERYONE TO ENJOY!
NONSENSE, YOUR MAJESTY. FAIRNESS HAS NOTHING TO DO WITH IT. THOSE PEASANTS HAVE PLENTY. THEY'RE JUST LAZY.
HEAR! HEAR!
SOUNDS LIKE A GOOD TAX TO ME!

TAPESTRIES, woven out of silk and wool, hung on castle walls to keep out drafts. One of the most famous from the Middle Ages is the Unicorn Tapestry series.

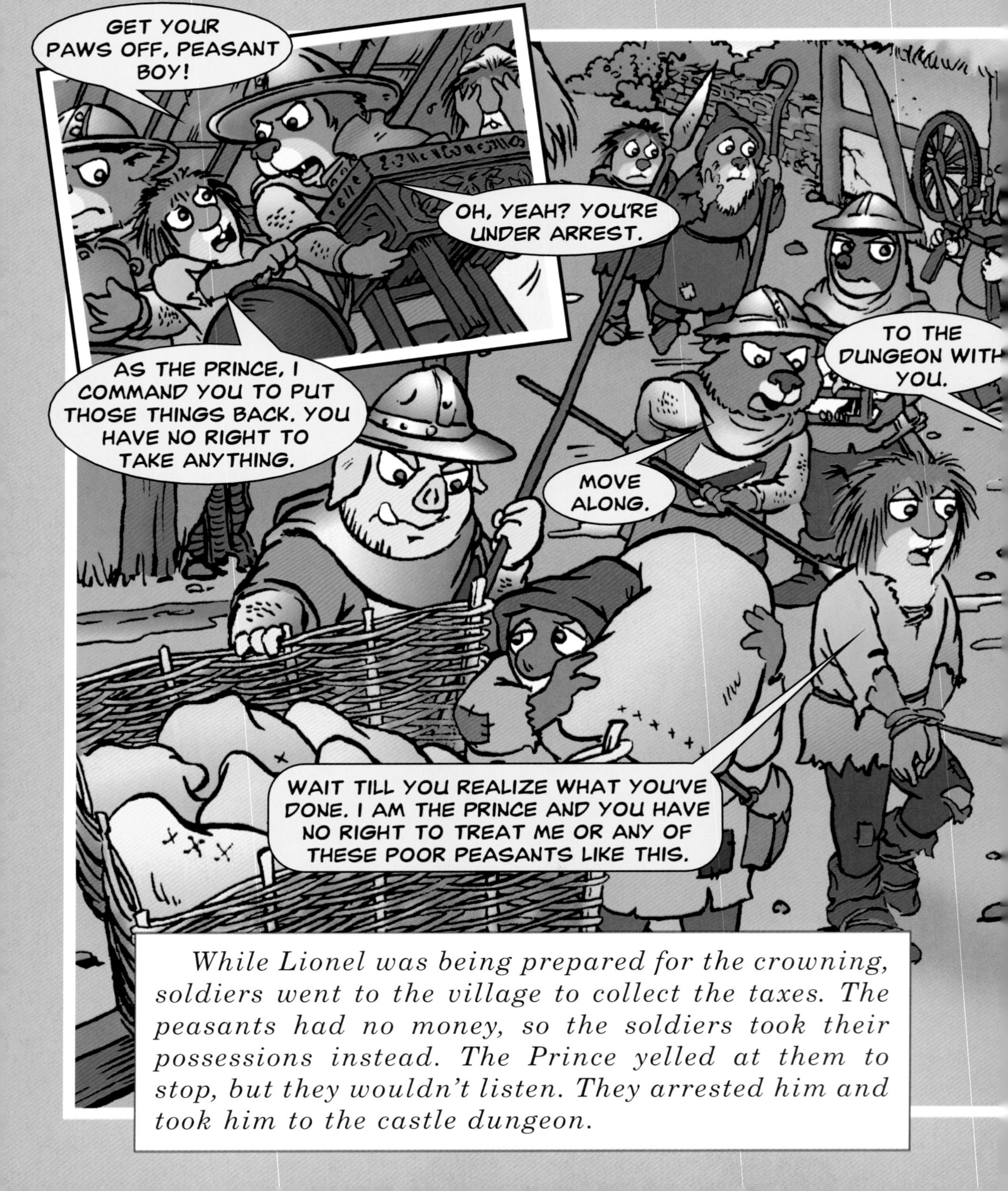
GET YOUR PAWS OFF, PEASANT BOY!
OH, YEAH? YOU'RE UNDER ARREST.
AS THE PRINCE, I COMMAND YOU TO PUT THOSE THINGS BACK. YOU HAVE NO RIGHT TO TAKE ANYTHING.
MOVE ALONG.
TO THE DUNGEON WITH YOU.
WAIT TILL YOU REALIZE WHAT YOU'VE DONE. I AM THE PRINCE AND YOU HAVE NO RIGHT TO TREAT ME OR ANY OF THESE POOR PEASANTS LIKE THIS.

While Lionel was being prepared for the crowning, soldiers went to the village to collect the taxes. The peasants had no money, so the soldiers took their possessions instead. The Prince yelled at them to stop, but they wouldn't listen. They arrested him and took him to the castle dungeon.

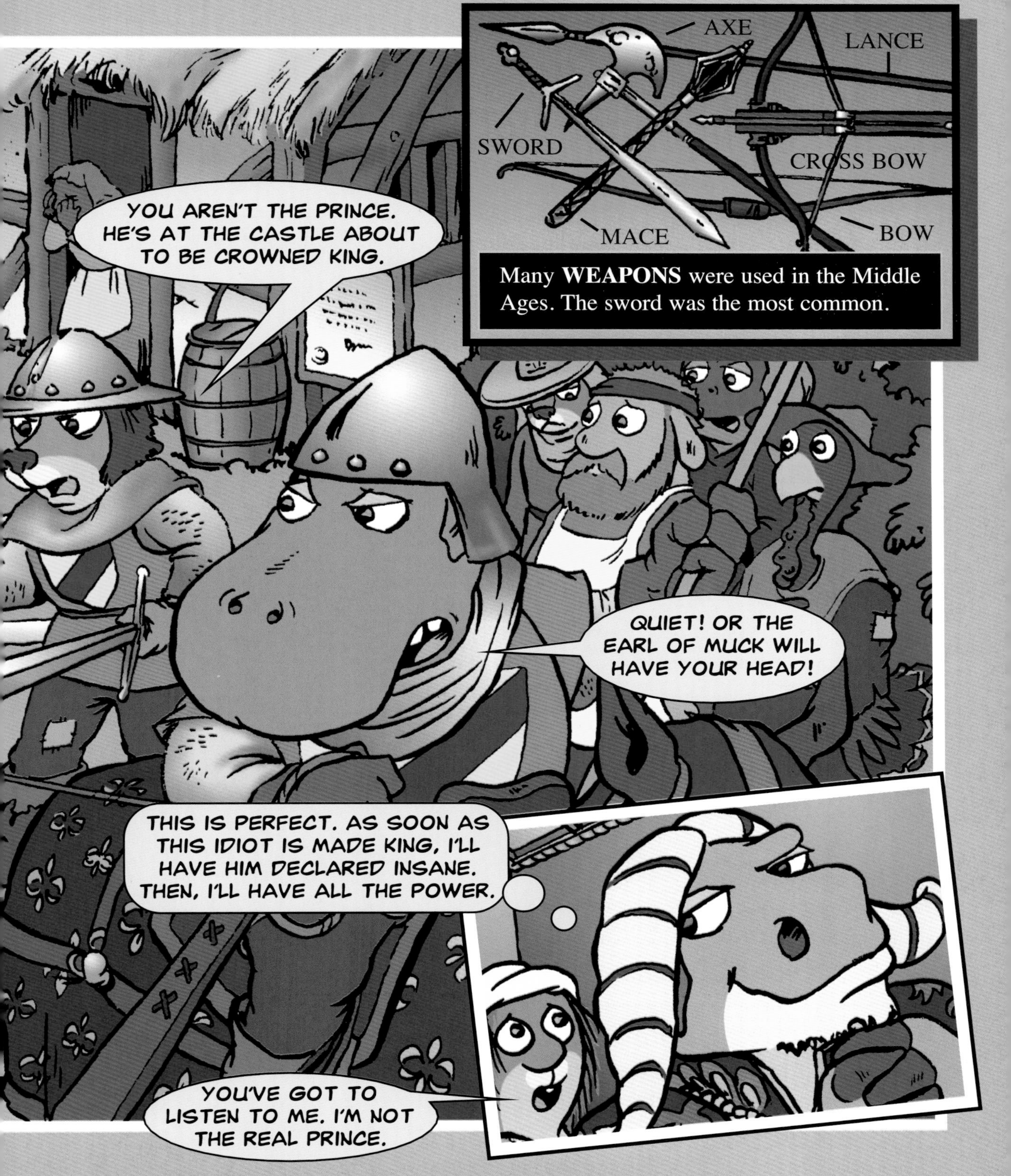
YOU AREN'T THE PRINCE. HE'S AT THE CASTLE ABOUT TO BE CROWNED KING.
AXE
LANCE
SWORD
CROSS BOW
MACE
BOW
Many **WEAPONS** were used in the Middle Ages. The sword was the most common.
QUIET! OR THE EARL OF MUCK WILL HAVE YOUR HEAD!
THIS IS PERFECT. AS SOON AS THIS IDIOT IS MADE KING, I'LL HAVE HIM DECLARED INSANE. THEN, I'LL HAVE ALL THE POWER.
YOU'VE GOT TO LISTEN TO ME. I'M NOT THE REAL PRINCE.

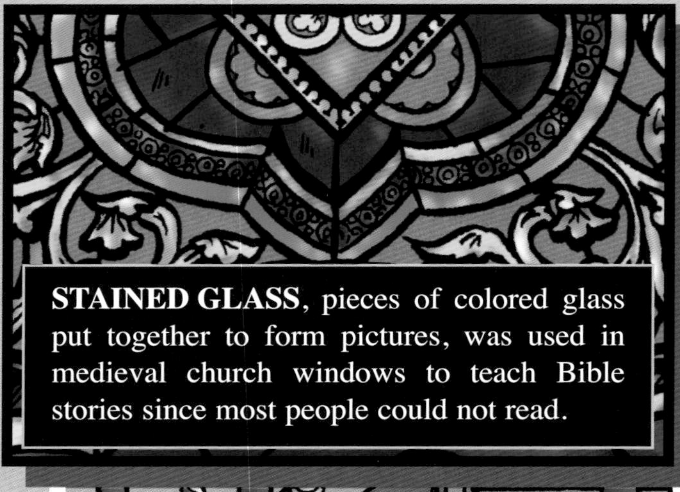

STAINED GLASS, pieces of colored glass put together to form pictures, was used in medieval church windows to teach Bible stories since most people could not read.

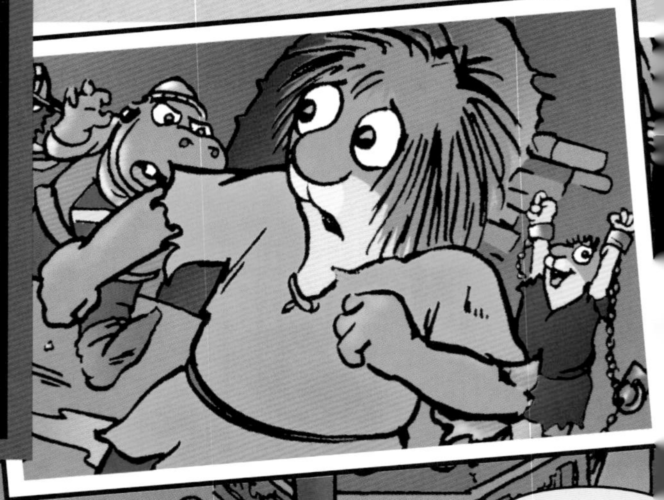

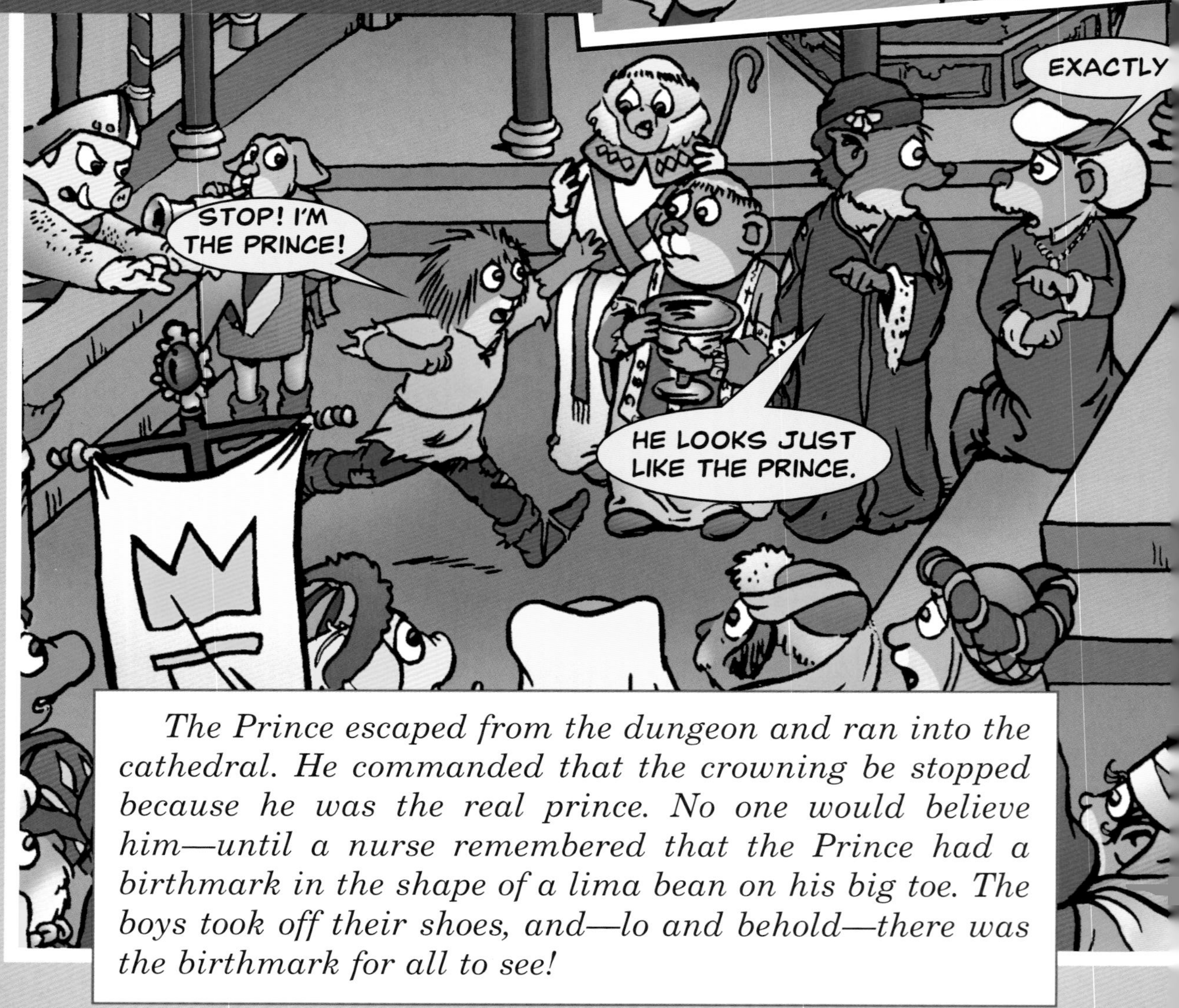
EXACTLY
STOP! I'M THE PRINCE!
HE LOOKS JUST LIKE THE PRINCE.

The Prince escaped from the dungeon and ran into the cathedral. He commanded that the crowning be stopped because he was the real prince. No one would believe him—until a nurse remembered that the Prince had a birthmark in the shape of a lima bean on his big toe. The boys took off their shoes, and—lo and behold—there was the birthmark for all to see!

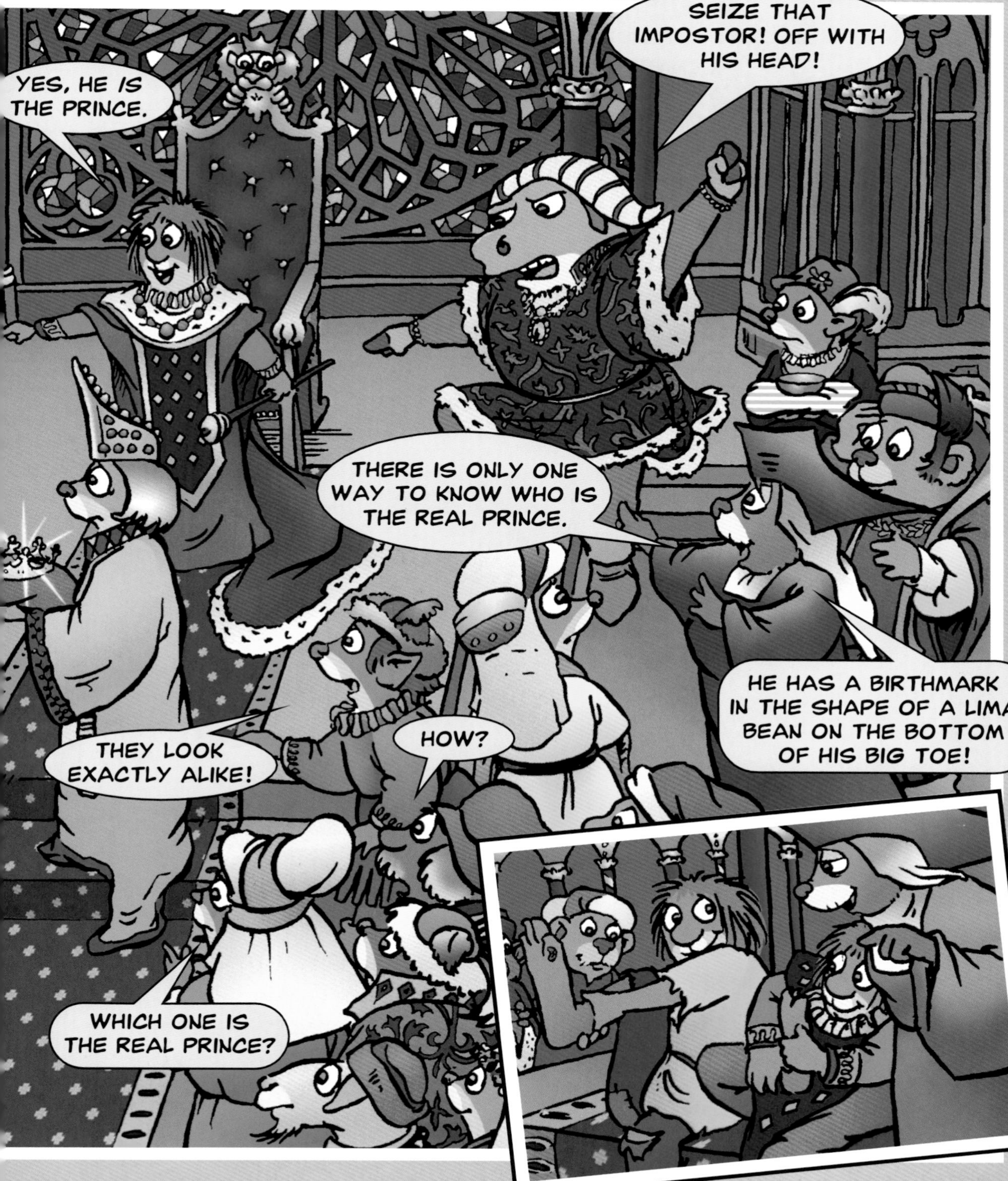
YES, HE IS THE PRINCE.
SEIZE THAT IMPOSTOR! OFF WITH HIS HEAD!
THERE IS ONLY ONE WAY TO KNOW WHO IS THE REAL PRINCE.
HE HAS A BIRTHMARK IN THE SHAPE OF A LIMA BEAN ON THE BOTTOM OF HIS BIG TOE!
THEY LOOK EXACTLY ALIKE!
HOW?
WHICH ONE IS THE REAL PRINCE?

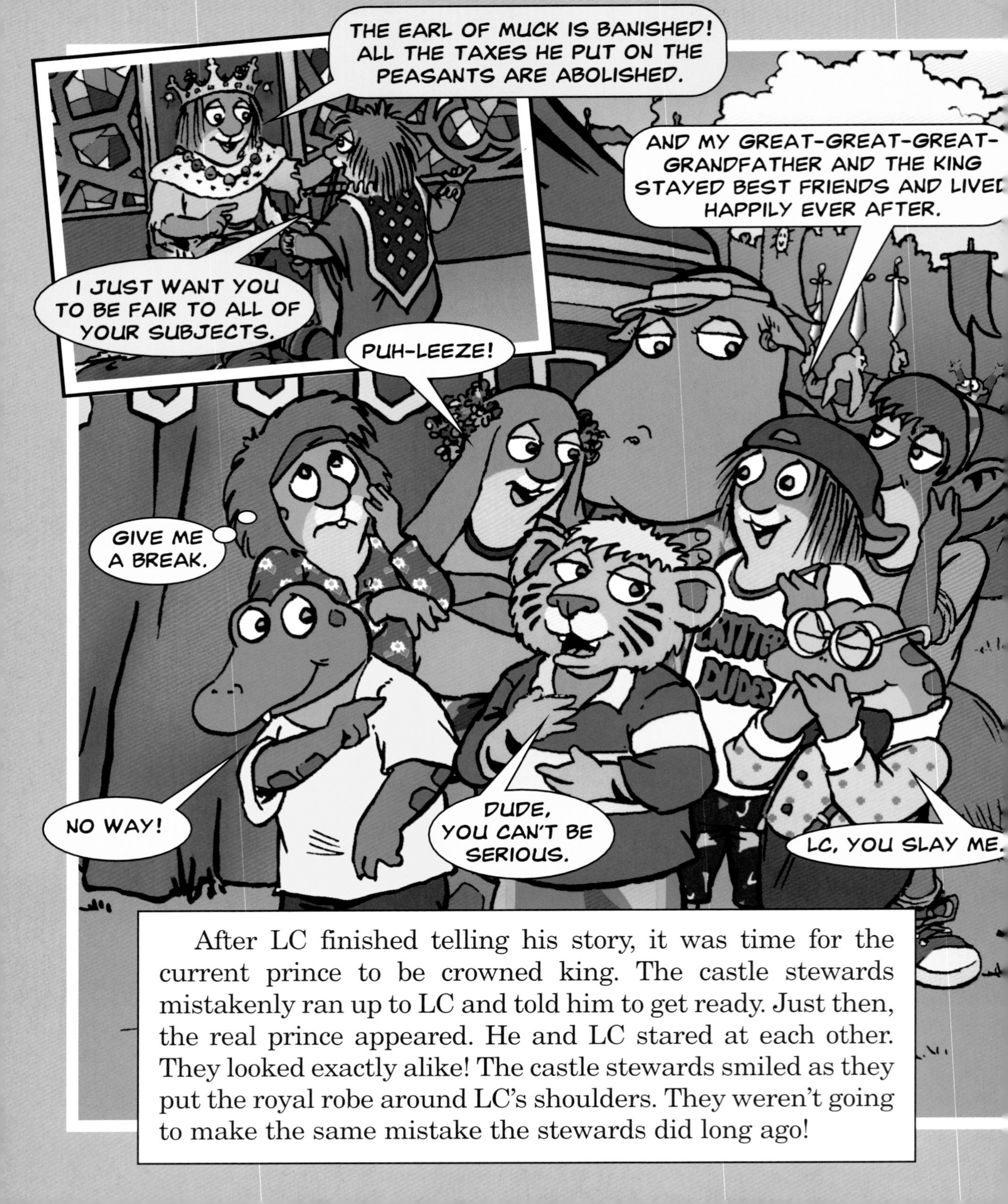
THE EARL OF MUCK IS BANISHED! ALL THE TAXES HE PUT ON THE PEASANTS ARE ABOLISHED.
I JUST WANT YOU TO BE FAIR TO ALL OF YOUR SUBJECTS.
AND MY GREAT-GREAT-GREAT-GRANDFATHER AND THE KING STAYED BEST FRIENDS AND LIVE
HAPPILY EVER AFTER.
PUH-LEEZE!
GIVE ME A BREAK.
NO WAY!
DUDE, YOU CAN'T BE SERIOUS.
LC, YOU SLAY ME.

After LC finished telling his story, it was time for the current prince to be crowned king. The castle stewards mistakenly ran up to LC and told him to get ready. Just then, the real prince appeared. He and LC stared at each other. They looked exactly alike! The castle stewards smiled as they put the royal robe around LC's shoulders. They weren't going to make the same mistake the stewards did long ago!

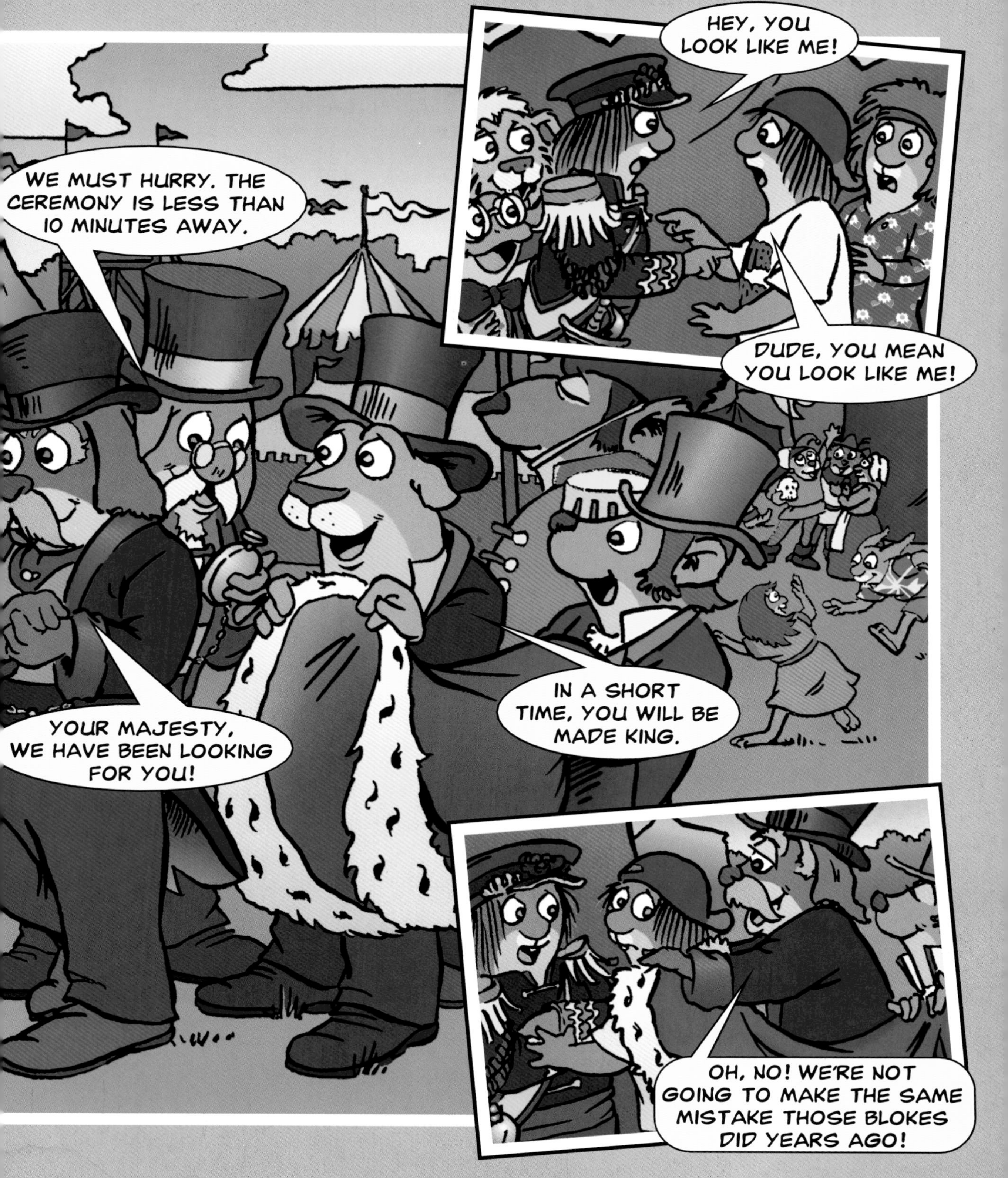
WE MUST HURRY. THE CEREMONY IS LESS THAN 10 MINUTES AWAY.
YOUR MAJESTY, WE HAVE BEEN LOOKING FOR YOU!
IN A SHORT TIME, YOU WILL BE MADE KING.
HEY, YOU LOOK LIKE ME!
DUDE, YOU MEAN YOU LOOK LIKE ME!
OH, NO! WE'RE NOT GOING TO MAKE THE SAME MISTAKE THOSE BLOKES DID YEARS AGO!

Vocabulary

abolished—outlawed, no longer allowed to happen. *After the Middle Ages, England abolished the extremely harsh dungeon punishments.*

addled—confused, unable to think clearly. *He was too addled to make any sense.*

banished—sent away to another place as a punishment. *In most fairy tales, the "bad guys" are banished from the kingdom.*

blokes—British slang for "guys" or "people."

bloodline—the features that are inherited from family ancestors. *The Golden retriever that won "best-of-show" at the National Dog Show came from a prize-winning bloodline.*

cathedral—a large, important church. *During the Middle Ages, important public announcements and events took place in a cathedral.*

chamber—an old-fashioned word for "bedroom." *During the Middle Ages, servants would prepare a noble person's chamber by lighting a fire in the fireplace to make it warm before sleeping.*

coronation—a ceremony when a king or ruler is crowned. *Fireworks and a large parade followed the coronation of the King of England.*

currant bun—a sweet roll made with small, dried seedless grapes. *Cinnamon-raisin bagels remind me of currant buns.*

mum—British word for "mom."

mutton—the meat of a fully grown sheep. *Mutton was a popular ingredient in stew during the Middle Ages.*

peasant—a member of a class of people who typically are farm workers. *During the Middle Ages, a peasant was typically a poor, uneducated farm worker.*

ranting and raving—yelling angrily and threatening. *His ranting and raving reminded me of a child having a temper tantrum.*

seize—to grab or take hold of something suddenly and with force. *The thief tried to seize the woman's handbag while running past her.*

stewards—people who act as officials or marshals at a large public event. *The castle stewards escorted the prince to his coronation ceremony.*

The Story and You

If you could look like someone else and lead their life for a day, who would it be? Explain why you chose this person and what you'd do for that day.

Would you like to have lived during the Middle Ages? Explain why or why not.

Do you think the story's ending is funny? Why or why not?